Lesson from a Madman!

"Gage, c'mon, take your turn."

An appalling silence now fell in the cabin. The girl thought she was going to scream as she watched the two men: Hog with his legs shaking, his face drained of color, his eyes bugging out of his bony head like a couple of eggs; and Striker, something like a snake, fascinating them both with a madness that terrified her.

"My turn is right now, Hog." And Striker drew his gun with a movement so fast neither of them could watch it ... "You goddam fool, Hog ... I got me a full loaded gun. And you—how many you got?" He started to laugh.

"But Striker, we was—we was just playing a game."

"Wrong! You was playing a game, Hog. Me, I never play games. I play for keeps." ... And Striker brought his big gun up and slammed him right across the side of his head ... while the girl stood there screaming.

Don't miss any of the lusty, hard-riding action in the Jove Western series, THE GUNSMITH

And coming next month:

THE GUNSMITH #72: DAUGHTER OF GOLD

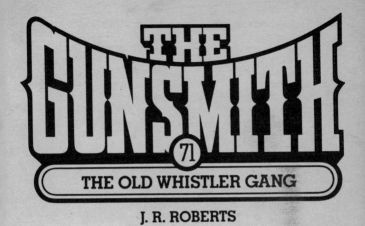

THE GUNSMITH
71
THE OLD WHISTLER GANG

J. R. ROBERTS

J

JOVE BOOKS, NEW YORK

THE GUNSMITH #71: THE OLD WHISTLER GANG

A Jove Book / published by arrangement with
the author

PRINTING HISTORY
Jove edition / November 1987

ISBN: 0-515-09217-7

Jove Books are published by The Berkley Publishing Group,
200 Madison Avenue, New York, New York, 10016.
The name "JOVE" and the "J" logo
are trademarks belonging to Jove Publications, Inc.

PRINTED IN THE UNITED STATES OF AMERICA

10 9 8 7 6 5 4 3 2 1

ONE

If anyone had asked Clint Adams what sort of woman he preferred he probably would have replied with the old adage, "The sort I happen to be with." Right now, he was looking down at the totally relaxed redhead who was lying beneath him, with her long legs still wrapped around his waist. Her eyes were closed, but she wasn't sleeping, only savoring the last drop of passion they had shared. As he shifted his weight, her legs fell away from him, and he withdrew from her wetness and lay down beside her. She'd still not opened her eyes, her breath coming evenly with the tempo of total satisfaction.

The Gunsmith studied the side of her face for a moment, then lay back and looked up at the ceiling of his hotel room. He felt wonderful. Yet strangely, he realized he wasn't thinking of the girl in bed beside him but of what had happened at the Pitchfork stage stop on his way into Bone City the day before. He had pulled in for a meal and to grain and water his horses: his team and Duke, his big black gelding, who was tied to the end gate of his gunsmithing wagon.

Clint Adams had never experienced anything like it. Neither, for that matter, had the Pitchfork agent, an aged, rheumy man; nor the two deputy marshals who had gotten off the stage with their

1

prisoner; and surely not the dark-haired, dark-eyed young woman also traveling in the coach.

The prisoner was a big man, and he was man-acled; obviously no one to take lightly. He and his companions were on their way to Cheyenne. Hog Wyatt was a man Clint Adams had heard a good deal of: an outlaw famous for his cruelty rather than his gunfighting expertise—though he was no amateur at that. Not very long ago, so Clint re-membered, Hog had tied one of his enemies to a corral pole and proceeded to shoot him slowly, that is, not delivering any fatal shot; wounding, but keeping his victim alive. At sundown, so the tale went, Hog had finally killed his man. He had then cut off both his ears and kept them. It was claimed he carried them in his pocket.

Clint had marked the white face of the girl; ash-white, evidently from the strain of riding with her fellow passengers. He had wondered why she hadn't changed to a later stage, but the thought hadn't stayed with him, for what happened shortly after drove everything else out of his mind.

Suddenly there was the sound of a horse coming up fast, and when one of the deputies stepped to the window he said over his shoulder, "Nothing. Just a woman riding in. In a hurry, I reckon."

"You sure? Anything else?" his fellow lawman had asked, still staying close to the prisoner.

"Sure," the first deputy replied.

In a moment the door burst open, and Clint Adams got his first shock. She couldn't have been thirty, and she was extremely attractive, though covered with a full-length duster—a trail driver's coat, which, though it concealed her figure, did nothing to conceal her spirit and her dancing green eyes under auburn hair.

"What kin we do fer you, miss?" the agent rasped, chomping on a fresh chaw of tobacco.

"I want to send a package on the next stage going to Bone City. Can you handle it?"

The agent spat copiously in the direction of a battered cuspidor, missing completely. " 'Course we kin handle it. That is for sure a dumb question. Where is it?"

"I've got it tied to my saddle skirt. I'll go get it." She turned to the door, saying over her shoulder, "Didn't know if you could handle it."

The Gunsmith was admiring fully the sensuous manner in which the girl moved, her sureness, and even the way she appeared slightly out of breath, which only added to her appeal. Yet there was something he couldn't quite put his finger on. And in the next instant he was to discover what that was.

She had moved closer to the door, with her hand starting to reach for the latch. The room had relaxed following the suddenness of her appearance. The agent wasn't even looking at her, one deputy had his eyes on the prisoner, who was staring at the wall, the other lawman was building himself a smoke with his tobacco and papers. The young passenger was staring at the newcomer, but with a sort of amazed look on her face.

Suddenly, quick as a cat, the girl in the trail coat turned, sweeping her long garment back and away from her to reveal her totally naked body; her prominent breasts bouncing right into the room. Naked except for the twin .45s strapped to her voluptuous thighs. In her hand she held a third side arm, and Clint noted that she was holding it in a way that told everyone present that she knew how to use it.

"The first one moves is dead." Her words were as hard as a gun barrel, as with her free hand she drew one of the Colts strapped to her thigh.

"I knew you'd make it, Honey," said the prisoner with a big grin on his face. "You got help?"

"Outside. Don't worry about it. The boys have run off their horses." She turned her attention to the two lawmen. "Unlock him. And be quick. And all of you drop your guns. You come outside too soon, you'll be cut off at the pockets!"

"Honey, I love ya!" Hog Wyatt was beaming all over. "Now close up that coat. You don't want to shock them any more than you got to."

Clint saw the eyes of the two deputies bugging out of their heads. And even the old curmudgeon of an agent had stirred. He was chewing faster than ever.

The girl tossed the Navy Colt to Hog and then drew the other and handed it to him as he stepped toward her. Clint had dropped his side arm as ordered, but he still had his belly gun under his shirt, tucked inside his belt.

"Honey, let's cut leather! That old geezer's been throwing his eyes at the clock; there could be a stage due!"

And they were gone.

And Clint Adams grinned now as he lay next to the girl in bed; grinned remembering the shock they'd all been left with.

The girl beside him stirred. "You dreamin'?" she asked.

"Maybe."

"Tell me about it."

"I'd rather show you," Clint said.

"That'd be all right, too."

He had run into her in the Elk Bar that afternoon and had taken an immediate liking. She'd invited him upstairs, but he'd said no, since he never paid for his pleasure they could go to his room at the hotel. It had thrown her a bit, but she hadn't hassled him; only telling him it would take a little time to work out an excuse with her boss. Which she did.

"I'm glad we came here," she whispered as he entered her again.

"I like it, too," Clint whispered back.

"Can we do it from behind?"

"Any way—all the ways—let's just play it as it comes."

And he flipped her over onto her hands and knees and mounted her high, hard, and deep.

Later, when he came downstairs after the girl had left, the room clerk handed him a note. He was surprised that anyone knew he was in Bone City, but when he saw the small, fine, obviously educated handwriting, he knew who it must be from. And he felt something stir happily inside him. Fine though the girl he'd picked up at the Elk Bar had turned out to be, she was not really his type. He liked her as he liked all women; but this young woman who signed herself Lorrie Everns was really his style. He'd surely been attracted to her at the Pitchfork stage stop, but he'd not really expected to see her again, assuming that she must be engaged in some other way since she had so resolutely kept to herself.

"Where is Mrs. Roman's Rooming House?" he asked the desk clerk.

The young man, a youth with pimples and bad breath, pointed down toward the livery where Clint had left Duke.

"Just before you get to the livery," he said. "It'll be on your right."

"Good enough," said the Gunsmith. He'd take a look at Duke and his team of horses to make sure the hostler was doing right by them and then he'd call on Miss Lorrie Everns.

It was undoubtedly Mrs. Roman herself who opened the door, the Gunsmith decided. Odd, he reflected, how you could tell a person's place almost without even knowing that was what you were doing. She was a big woman with a big bosom; big, bare, doughy forearms, and big hands that she held together at her waist.

"It's Mister Adams, is it? I'll tell Miss Everns that you'll be in the parlor."

He was seated only a few moments when she appeared in the doorway. She seemed a little breathless, as though she'd hurried, not wanting to keep him waiting. Or, he wondered, perhaps she was like that anyway.

"As you see, I received your note."

"It's good of you to come. Let me . . . let me just catch my breath for a moment. Would you like some coffee or tea?"

"Only if you're having something."

"I'll just put the kettle on. Mrs. Roman is very hospitable and has allowed me the use of her kitchen. I'll only be a moment."

He relaxed while she disappeared into another part of the house, still thinking about the adventure at the Pitchfork stage stop. Hog Wyatt. Good that he hadn't known he was the Gunsmith. Crazy man like that could easily want to try for a reputation. And this reminded Clint of how much he disliked the publicity of being known as a gunslinger. The name was a true one, for his profession was indeed gunsmithing. But the Eastern papers and fancy journals had taken him up as a gunfighter. Well, his friend Hickok had had the same problem. But Bill wasn't around anymore to tell about it. Clint was still mulling this over when Lorrie Everns came in with a tray of tea things.

"Are you recovered from all your adventures on the trail?" he asked.

She smiled a little at that, looking down and then at him. "I believe so. It was a bit of a shock, you know. First of all, to have this criminal riding in the same coach and then that woman. Heavens!" And she looked away, her cheeks coloring.

Clint Adams thought she looked delightful. He was particularly taken by a soft brown curl that came around her left earlobe into her ear. And her brown eyes were like wells.

"Good tea," he said. "What can I do for you, Miss Everns? You said you wanted to talk to me. You don't look like the sort who goes in for guns, and you might or might not know that my trade is gunsmithing."

She was looking at him a little nervously now. "One of those marshals told me you were a former lawman, and yes, that you knew a lot about guns, but. . . ."

"But he meant shooting them, didn't he?"

"Yes, he did. But. . . ."

"Well, I have been a lawman, and I do have a sort of reputation with shooting, but my business is fixing guns."

"I wondered if you might be able to help me. I have a little money and I could pay you."

He thought she looked like a deer. Her ears turned in just a little at the tops, and she had the freshness of the timber and meadow about her.

"Might I ask where you're from?"

"From Indiana. A small town, I'm sure you've never heard of it."

He didn't press her, but said, "The reason I ask is, you give the feeling of a person brought up on the land."

"Oh, yes!" And she smiled at him suddenly without any holding back.

In a moment, her face darkened. "I wanted to ask you to help me with something."

"Well, I'll have to hear about it before I can tell you if I can help you."

She looked down at her hands, which were lying in her lap. She began to speak without looking up, addressing her folded hands.

"It's my brother, Abel. He's just a boy. Just seventeen. A good boy. Our . . . Mother died almost a year ago, and I've sort of been, well, I have been the head of the household."

"What about your father?" Clint asked the

question carefully, feeling that the problem might well be there. And he was right.

"That's just what I'm concerned about," she said, lifting her eyes to his. "Our father—well, neither of us know much of anything about him. You see, he left while I was still very young, and Abel even younger. Mother wouldn't say anything when we asked, so we finally stopped asking."

"Is he still alive?"

"I don't know. And I don't know if he's—if he's not."

Clint understood the difficulty she was having as he watched her struggle. "Maybe just talk, tell it as it comes," he suggested mildly.

"We neither of us really remember—Abel or myself. I have a vague memory of someone, a man, when I was very small, and I've always supposed it was my dad. But we don't have any history on him. He came out west it seems. Mother said he left in order to find a place, and then he was going to send for us. I do remember a few things when I was maybe seven or eight. It's a good memory. I—I must have loved him. Anyhow, I want to find out what happened. And so does Abel. You see, he just disappeared. Mother talked about it a little at first, and then she stopped. I guess she gave up. She wrote him somewhere, but she never received any answer. And then she stopped mentioning him at all. You know, I can sort of see him in my mind; but then, I don't know. It's all so vague and seems so long ago. All I know is that when Mother died last year, I decided I wanted to come out here and see if there was anything. . . ."

"But do you know where exactly? Is it Bone City? Did you write to the authorities? The law?"

"Mother did. And I did, too. Privately. Nothing came back. Nothing. That is, I did receive two letters saying simply that there was no trace of anyone by that name."

"He could have changed his name."

"I know. I know, and that is what I think Mother was afraid of. Afraid he might have gotten into some kind of trouble."

"But you're beginning to think that's what happened. That maybe he hit the owlhoot trail."

"Owlhoot?"

"Outlaw."

"I see."

"I'm sorry," he said quickly, seeing her reaction. "But if you want me to help you find out what happened to your father, we'll have to consider every possibility."

"It's all right. I understand. And I thank you." Her eyes searched his face. "Will you help me? I would pay you for your time and trouble."

"Where does your brother fit in here? You began by saying you wanted to speak to me about him."

"Abel and I talked it over, and we agreed that I would come out here first and see if there was anything that would tell us where he might be or what might have happened to him. If I got any news of Dad then I was to send for Abel. But. . . ."

"But Abel decided to come out on his own."

She nodded. "That's just it. One day I found him gone. He left me a note saying what he was doing, that it was not my job to come out to Wyoming, but he was going to do it, and he would send for me if he discovered anything at all."

"Do you have any idea where Abel is now?"

"None." She shook her head. "He is a very stubborn boy." She bit her lower lip as she thought about it and then said, "I've got to find Abel. He's very strong-headed. If you could help me?"

"But you think he's around Bone City?"

"It's a name our mother mentioned—a funny name, and the kind that sticks in the memory. Another time she mentioned somebody named Conrad, I don't know if that was his first or last name. And then . . . a place named, I think, Kilton—something like that. I haven't found it on any map, and nobody I've asked around here has ever heard of the place."

Clint was shaking his head slowly. "None of those names are familiar to me. Look, I'll be glad to help you if I can. I'll ask around, have a look-see. But I can't promise a thing. I mean, we're talking about a long time ago."

She sighed softly. "Yes, a long time ago."

"Although maybe not so long ago out here," he added. "A long time ago for you and your brother back in Indiana. But your father could have been here just recently." He leaned forward a little. "What was his name?"

"Andrew . . . Andrew—Andy Everns. I'd guess he'd be in his early fifties now."

She stood up. "Mr. Adams, I want to give you some money now, on account."

He had come to his feet with her. "Please, let

that wait. Let's see what I can do, and then we'll talk about that. I assure you it's nothing to make a few inquiries. And call me Clint.''

He wanted to stay with her longer, to hold her in conversation; she delighted him. But he knew it was painful for her, and realized it was much better to keep things on a business basis, for the present. A moment for socializing could appear later when she was not so gripped with the search for her father and her feisty young brother.

His thoughts were full of Lorrie Everns as he walked toward his hotel. And he was thinking, too, of the name Conrad. Somehow that name suddenly did have a familiar ring to it.

TWO

In the high Rockies of western Wyoming the snow remained all through the summer months, shouldering the strong peaks in sparkling white against the soaring sky. Along the mountains, in the long green valleys, elk and antelope grazed, and in the tall timber and hidden meadows there was rich game. And there were wild horses; marvelously free beasts never touched by rope or the hand of man. This land was clean. The days and nights were always new; the air crisp as a minted coin.

For the man astride the big black gelding there was hardly a place like it, even in the West. And it was one of the reasons why he had never gone back East, where he had come from. Clint Adams was a man with the wanderlust, but he was also a man who never wanted to be anywhere, except where he was at any particular moment. A man who lived in the here and now. Like a number of men who had to live by the gun, he'd found that attitude a first necessity. And thus far in his young life he had never regretted it.

A man in his prime, six feet plus an inch, slim, and well built, carrying a scar on the left side of his face from a stone chip kicked up by a bullet. Women found him handsome; men found him squarely honest, with no nonsense about him.

As always, he rode now straight in the saddle,
yet with an obvious grace of movement, and with
an alertness not only in his eyes but all the way
through him.

"Well, big fella, which way?" Duke, the big
black horse who was as much friend as animal
servant to Clint Adams, twitched his big ears and
ducked his head against a cruising deer fly.

The Gunsmith squinted up toward the rimrocks, then let his eyes move down through the
long sweep of land that ran all the way down to
the Greybull River. Overhead an eagle swept the
sky, and the sun bore down on the man and horse.
Somehow he had simply decided to ride out in the
direction of Jack Creek, which, according to the
old hostler at the livery, ran just below the big
rock promontory known as Shoshone Peak.

Clint was not really familiar with the country.
He'd been in Bone City years ago, but he'd never
ridden up toward the North Fork of the Greybull,
and yet something had drawn him. What? The
name Conrad? And then . . . something about
another name . . . Kilton, the girl had mentioned.
A place. Why was Conrad familiar to him, Kilton
less so, but still with something pulling at him?

Indeed, it was really why he'd walked down to
the livery that morning and saddled Duke and ridden out. It was a way he had at times, when he
wanted to think, to study some problem, and
Duke was without question a horse to talk things
over with.

That night he made his bed on pine needles at
the edge of a pocket meadow high up near the rimrocks. Conrad? Henry? Charles? Ben? He went

through the entire alphabet trying to put a first name in front of Conrad; then he tried last names. Billings? Johannsen? Taggart? He gave up, knowing it had to work in him, like a splinter in your thumb that would sooner or later work its way out through the skin.

He lay on his bedroll on the soft pine needles, smelling the spruce and fir and pine, and when the wind stirred now and again, he smelled Duke. And he listened to the night sounds in the high timber around him and in the earth and sky. He slept then, but not deeply, for on the trail he always slept half awake. It was, again, one of the necessities.

At dawn he came instantly awake. He waited, watching the first rays of the sun. He rose and rolled his blankets and his ground cover. He stood silent for some moments in the cool, pure morning air. He built a small fire and boiled coffee. And it had come to him then. Conrad. Clarence Conrad.

Conrad had just finished his evening chores when the stranger rode up the trail on the blue roan. He had been watching the horse and rider since they had passed the butte down at the entrance to the basin. Conrad stood now outside the round horse corral with the shotgun in his hand, a tall, gaunt man, with the skin on his face and neck and hands and wrists criss-crossed and leathery from all the seasons of his sixty years spent in the shadow of the Big Horn Mountains.

The stranger rode up slowly, passing the stand of pine by the spring box without looking either to left or right. He rode right to the corral and dis-

mounted, nodding to Conrad, who was still holding the shotgun. He was a good deal younger than
the rancher had at first thought, only seventeen
maybe, or even less; a boy. And judging from the
way he handled the roan, obviously a greener. He
surely was not from this part of the country. Certainly not the man Conrad had been expecting.
Still, Conrad did not wholly relax his vigilance.

"What kin I do for you, young feller?" the
rancher asked.

And now, studying the boy—his bony features,
deepset brown eyes, his lanky, loose movements as
he stepped down from the roan and took a couple
of steps forward—Conrad felt something stir in
him. His alertness swept through him, along with
a feeling of uneasiness, even danger. What was it
with this young man, this boy—a kid, really—
standing there with his hands at his sides, standing
easy, but solid, too, all inside himself, his brown
eyes steady and clear and paying full attention to
the man he was looking at.

"I'm looking for a man named Conrad," the
boy said. "They told me in town to come here."

"Riddle Rock?"

"Yeah."

Conrad's thoughts touched the questioning in
himself, and he tried to find words to put his mind
at ease. He knew the boy wasn't looking for work.
He sure wasn't a hand for this part of the country.
Not that he wasn't handy. That was clear in the
way he stood, the way he moved and looked at
things. Yet he was still green to the country, for
sure.

Conrad's eyes swept past the visitor to the field

of bunch grass and lower down, sage brush; and the big butte below, at the start of the trail down to the valley, and up which the young boy had ridden. And he felt his grip tighten on the shotgun.

"You see anyone on your way up here, boy? Any rider?"

"No. I didn't see anyone."

"Where you from, boy? I know you ain't from this part of the country."

"Indiana. Back East. I came out here looking for this man, Conrad."

The uneasiness in the older man was spreading. He looked toward the house, suddenly remembering the spring when he and Aaron Whistler had cut the logs, snaked them down from up by the rimrock, and then built the cabin.

"That is a long way to travel," he said. "Just to see a man. What you want with him?"

"When I see him I'll tell him." The boy was respectful, and he had the dignity of the lonely.

Conrad's eyes went to the log house again. With his right hand he scratched the stubble on his big, square jaw. The hand was a claw, the fingers bent to the palm. He was thinking of Aaron Whistler lying in the mud of Riddle Rock with a bullet in his back and himself with a bullet through his gun hand, hunting the killer for more than a week with the biggest posse ever formed in that country. Fifteen years ago. And the whole of the Territory in arms over the coldblooded murder of one of the West's most famous gunmen. In those days, Conrad could remember, no one favored bushwhacking, even less than they did now.

And he could still hear Striker's promise to

come back from prison and finish the job.

"A man with a gun never retires," Whistler had once told him. "No matter what side of the law. He dies just like he lived."

With his gun hand crippled Conrad had had to retire. But now, all these years later, with Striker's escape from Laramie, he suddenly realized he'd have a chance to test the truth of Aaron Whistler's remark.

It was just now, following this train of thought that his uneasiness found words. For it was in the boy's stance, the way he stood planted right there before him, almost as though growing right out of the ground.

And it was fate, Conrad told himself, his coming at such a time. For it couldn't have been a worse time. Yet, this was the way it was meant to be, and there was nothing he could do but accept it. Though he had made his promise, and he would keep it.

"I am Conrad," he said at last.

"I'm Abel Everns."

"What kin I do for you?"

Knowing the boy, who he was, Conrad now understood the simplicity and directness of his next sentence.

"Did you know my father?"

Conrad looked at him, studying the answer he would give. He spat in the direction of a pile of dried horse manure. Then he said, "Can't say as how I ever knowed a man name of Everns."

"Maybe twelve, fifteen years back."

Conrad spat again, in the same direction as before, his eyes going quickly to the trail up which the boy had ridden. "Nope."

They looked at each other for a moment. Conrad saw the boy weighing him, not sure where the truth was, maybe.

"I came a long way looking for you," the boy said. "I wanted to talk to somebody who knew my father. I never saw him, never laid eyes on him."

Conrad was looking toward the trail again. It was four, five days since Striker's escape. His eyes swung back to the boy.

"How come you figure I knowed your Pa?"

"He knew a man named Conrad."

"There is others with that name."

"Not around Bone City."

"Thought you said you came from Riddle Rock."

"I did. Got off the stage there since it's the next town near to Bone City. That close, I figure my dad could've been in either place, or the both."

"I don't know him. I don't recollect anyone by that name—Everns is it?"

The boy shoved his hands into the pockets of his denims. "Maybe his name wasn't Everns. I've been thinking about that. They told me in town you used to be marshal in Riddle Rock, a long time back. Maybe my dad was—maybe he did something. Long ago," he added softly.

"Then what you want to know for?" Conrad's voice was sharp.

"I want to know. I've got to know. I just got to!" The boy's words were harsh with his need. His eyes gripped Conrad. "Can't you think of someone you knew around here then, maybe not all that long ago, maybe someone looked some like me. Somebody now maybe your age?"

"What about your Ma?" Conrad asked suddenly.

The boy shoved his hands deeper into his pockets. "She died a year ago. I worked a year to save money to come out here. Part-time work," he added.

"Didn't she tell you about your Paw? Was he out here by himself, what I mean?"

The boy looked down at his feet, then at Conrad. "She'd never talk about him and never wanted me to, neither. Only that time me and my sister heard her talking to somebody—a friend—about my dad; how he'd written her saying something about someone named Conrad, and Bone City."

Conrad studied him a moment. "Could be as how your Paw wanted it left that way, boy."

"I don't even know for sure if he's dead. Could be he's still alive."

They were silent, the boy's question and the man's refusal lying stiff between them.

"Can you help me?" the boy said at last.

And after a moment Conrad said, "Put your horse in the barn. There's oats in the bin. Come on up to the house then. It'll be time to eat."

Abel Everns turned away then, feeling something strange inside him, and led the roan into the log barn. As they entered, a pack rat scurried for cover. The roan whickered as he smelled the grain.

Abel stripped him, put a rope halter on him, and poured feed into the wooden box. While the roan chomped the oats, he rubbed him down with some sacking he found on a bench. Then he

walked up to the house where the man was standing on the porch with his shotgun.

Their horses were tiring, for they had pushed
them. The two riders felt it to be especially so as
they crossed the tawny plain between the high
benchland and the big butte. It was the forenoon
now and the dry, brittle buffalo grass was snap-
ping under the extreme heat. The girl was on the
point of calling for a stop when Hog Wyatt drew
rein. He was riding a dappled gray horse; sturdy,
but starting to blow.

"Can't we get out of this heat?" Honey said,
wiping her forehead with the back of her wrist.

Hog watched her wet silk shirt clinging around
her nipples, and in spite of his fatigue, felt his passion rising. They had stopped only once in their
flight to satiate themselves, while at the same time
giving the horses a rest and then had pressed on.

"We'll walk 'em a little," Hog said. "Yonder
by them trees we'll head into the high ground."

"Is that where we aim to hide out?"

He nodded.

"Shit, we bin circling back a whole lot," Honey
said, and there was irritation in her voice.

"I know that," he snapped. "But I am aiming
to cover our tracks."

They were walking their horses now, and
Honey's sorrel began shaking its head against its
mane, which had gotten tangled in the wide
Mexican headstall. The girl reached forward and
began freeing the long flaxen hair where it had
wrapped around the leather.

"We'll make it soon," Hog said.

"Afternoon?"

"Sure."

The sun beat down even more viciously, burning through their hats, their shirts, the backs of their hands, enclosing them in a fist of stifling heat.

"Them fucking marshals ain't gonna bother us," Hog said, relishing the words that he'd already said to her at least a half dozen times. "Not that one, anyways. I'll get that other soon enough, too."

"Might caution some not to cut our trail," Honey said. Her green eyes were large and her breasts high and firm, upon which Hog was now feasting his own hungry orbs.

"Wish there was shade," he said.

"Same here."

"We could have us a little bit of fun."

"It's hot."

"I'm hot in my pants," Hog said.

"So'm I."

"We'll get to the box canyon soon. Then we'll be safe. There ain't a man alive can find that place."

"How come you found it?" the girl asked a couple of hours later as they approached the sheer rock wall, sparsely dotted with shrubbery and some small trees.

"I got showed it," Hog said. "It used to be, and I reckon it still is, the perfect hideout. On account of nobody knows anything about it."

And she could see as they rode through the narrow opening in the rock, which was hidden with natural growth, that no one could possibly stumble onto the place. It was really a slit in the high rock, and now the slit widened as the trail twisted and they rode into a high box canyon.

"By God, it is a box!" the girl exclaimed. Three sides of the canyon, and almost all of the fourth side were solid rock, and extremely high.

"There're a lot of them in this here country," Hog explained. "They, like, make a natural corral. Good for running in wild horses. I don't believe there be any better'n' this here."

They were both feeling hopeful as they rode their tired horses across the floor of the canyon, which was spotted with little carpets of lush grass. Toward the far end, a stand of cottonwoods ran into box elders and willows. There was a small creek.

"Plenty of feed, water, even game. A man could live here this good while," Hog said proudly.

"Then screw those lawmen," she said exuberantly.

"No," Hog said, with humorous severity. "You screw me. And don't you forget it!"

She turned her head to measure him with a cool glance. "And don't you forget it, neither, Hog!"

He turned away from her and spat viciously at a clump of grass.

They were silent now as they entered the stand of trees and picked up a game trail that began leading them up a high rise that Hog said would break out into a plateau still within the box canyon, and from which they would have a commanding view of anyone entering the hideout. Not to mention the advantage in any passage at arms that night become necessary.

"And nobody knows!" Honey couldn't get over it. "That's the beauty of it, ain't it! Nobody knows!"

And he nodded. His irritation with her aggression had not left.

"Nobody," Hog said. "Nobody even bin here by the looks of things in one hell of a time. 'Course, back in the old days this here place was bustling. Robbers' Roost it was. We was the best, by God!" His eyes gleamed. "But never mind about that. . . ."

And he fell suddenly silent, as though remembering something, maybe something like he shouldn't be talking, the girl thought. And she wondered.

"You used to be here?" she said, for she wasn't one to fear asking a question now and again. She'd heard him mention "the old days," though rarely. Those must have been high old times, she decided.

"Used to—with the boys."

They were silent again as they stopped at a thin stream and let their horses drink.

Although it was still midafternoon, the sun was reaching low on the top of the canyon wall and throwing shadows below. The girl thought how it was going to be getting dark early.

"Should be that cabin here still," Hog said.

"Cabin?" Her eyes lit up, and she realized how tired she was.

"Was built solid. Ought to still be here, but 'course that was some good while ago."

"How long?"

"Maybe fifteen years. Like that."

Her mood fell. "Could've burned down. Nobody was here in all that time?" she asked as they stepped their horses across the stream.

"Only feller could be, he's in the pen for life. And myself. And I was out of this here country." He had left when the gang had broken up, and gone to Texas—GTT, as the saying had it. And a good thing. The law had made a pretty damn clean sweep when they busted the old gang.

They had been following a game trail, and there were deer droppings and also bear signs easily recognizable.

"We'll have game," Honey said. "How far now?"

"Just yonder," he said.

And in only a few moments they had nearly lost the trail, for it was almost completely overgrown. Hog was off his horse and she had followed suit, the trail being all but impassable. Slowly, carefully they led their horses, Hog in the lead, picking out the almost invisible trail.

"Nothing but deer and bear been in here," he muttered.

And then suddenly they broke out of the brush and came into a clearing at one end of which stood a log cabin.

"There she be," Hog said, victory in his voice. "I told ya!"

Honey gave a little laugh as she drew next to him where he had stopped to gaze at the cabin.

"That sonofabitch was built to last," he said.

There was a horse corral, but some of the poles were down, and there was a collapsed lean-to at one end of the cabin.

"We'll take it slow here for a spell, then move on down country," Hog said. "Give the law time to cool down."

"They'll soon get tired of looking for us." Honey was smiling as she touched his arm.

His hand reached over and began to fondle her buttocks.

"By God," he said admiringly. "There ain't a fucking man, woman, or broke hoss within miles and miles of this place." He spat appreciatively into a loose clump of sage. "I'll strip the horses and you can wrangle some grub."

"We'll maybe need firewood," she said.

"Used to be a box of it inside. Nobody never left the place without filling it." He chuckled. "If they did . . . !" He made a slicing gesture with his forefinger across his throat and laughed.

"Hurry up," Honey said as he took her horse's reins. "We might want to see how the bunk is first."

He grinned at her, his passion heating in his trousers. "Might, by God!"

They had just started to move apart from each other when the voice came from beyond the corral where there was a clump of bullberry bushes.

"You can just hold it right there!"

Hog Wyatt spun, his hand dropping to his gun as the girl jumped away from him and dropped to the ground.

But that voice wasn't fooling, nor was the bullet

that struck the heel of Hog's boot.

"Next one will be your left ball, Hog!" The voice was as hard and implacable as that bullet in his boot heel. Hog Wyatt froze.

"Don't move even a eyelash," he said to the girl. "He can shoot a button off your shirt without burning the cloth."

They both caught the rich chuckle breaking from the far side of the corral.

The Gunsmith knew it when he watched Duke's ears. The big black had suddenly stopped chomping the buffalo grass and lifted his head, his ears straight up, then moving forward, then a little to the side, then again up in a diagonal as his eyes went to the timberline.

"Good, big fella," Clint said softly. He moved suddenly and with all the speed he could get under him as he dove for the nearby willows. Hidden now, he rose carefully to a crouching position, pausing each moment to listen. He took plenty of time changing his position. Finally, he was standing.

Duke was still not feeding on the buffalo grass, but kept his head up, his eyes rolling a little, and his ears still forward and up, listening.

Clint Adams had been listening, too. And there was something strange. He could hear the jangle of a bit now, and in a moment he smelled the horse as the wind shifted.

He was well hidden when the little hammerhead sorrel broke out of the trees and headed with a whinny toward Duke. There was a rider, but he was slumped over his saddle horn and about to fall. And in a moment he did. His boot caught in the stirrup and he was dragged as the sorrel spooked.

With a soft word to Duke, Clint began edging toward the sorrel, who was rolling its eyes and bobbing its head back toward the man whose foot was caught in the stirrup. It took a while but with coaxing, talking softly to both Duke and the sorrel, Clint finally managed to put a hand on the animal's neck. He gentled him with his hands and with words, finally managing to free the hung-up horseman, who was clearly dead. As his leg dropped away from the stirrup that had held him, he lay on his back in the meadow, fully exposed. Snorting, his former mount sidled away, eyes rolling, and finally dropped his head to the grass to graze.

It only took the Gunsmith a moment to recognize who the rider was, as he stared down into the face of one of the two marshals who had been escorting Hog Wyatt to prison. And he'd been dead more than a little while.

THREE

Conrad had finished cleaning the Winchester. From time to time his eyes had gone to the trail, the horizon, the long sweeping valley of the Greybull stretching below. He put the rifle down now, after checking its action, and leaned back in his chair on the porch of the cabin, once again allowing his eyes to stretch over the long vista of grass and rock, down past the big butte, and on toward the Greybull rushing south through the lower country.

He reached down and drew the six-gun from the holster that was lying on the wooden floor at his feet. It was an old Navy Colt, with a long, dark blue barrel, and generally it hung in its worn, hand-tooled holster from a peg by the fireplace in the main room of the cabin. It was not his. In the late afternoon he had taken it from its peg and brought it out to the porch to clean. Not that he ever used it. He was still awkward with his left hand, except with the shotgun, and given time, with the rifle. But he knew he was going to need all the armaments he could muster.

"What are you going to tell him?" Nellie had asked when he'd told her who the boy was. Abel Everns had been feeding his horse.

She was a thin woman with black hair tied in a knot in back, and she had red, scuffed hands.

"I ain't gonna tell him nothing," he'd answered.

"He can find out."

"Nobody knows but you and me," he'd said. "Nan don't know."

The mother had turned her head to make sure their daughter was out of earshot.

"What's he look like?"

"Like him."

She was silent with her thoughts. Conrad, knowing her so many years, could almost read her mind.

"I give my promise, Nell."

She looked up at him with her eyes wide, the way she did those few times when she really wanted something.

"You're not going to send him away."

"I got to." And he had looked at a splinter in his thumb to avoid her eyes.

"But he's got no folks. No place to go."

"Ain't our business."

"I figure it is. A boy should have folks, a home. We could use a hand. He don't have to find out."

"I give my promise."

"I know he made you promise, but you can't always tell what a man means by just his words."

He had never before refused her on the rare times she wanted something. But he was thinking of Striker. And Striker had made *him* a promise.

"No," he had said finally. "He has got to go."

And after he'd eaten dinner the boy had ridden away.

Conrad closed the chamber of the six-gun and wiped his hands on the cleaning rag. The sun had dropped down behind the far rimrocks, and the sky, though still light, had taken on the soft velvet it so often had at that time of year when it was getting to be dark.

With the cool that now sharpened the day he could smell the horses differently as they cropped the grass near the cabin. He was thinking how long it would take Striker to come back to his old haunts hunting for him. Well, he would be here. He would try to be ready. He, by God, would be ready!

"Sonofabitch. . . ." The words came as one, soft but clear from the tight line of Deputy Marshal Lije Delehanty's lips as he looked down at his dead partner lying on the bench at the undertaker's in Bone City.

The undertaker, a thin man with low-hanging trousers, a big longhorn mustache, and a lazy look in his narrow face stood silently as Delehanty uttered those well-used words.

Clint Adams had brought the dead man in, tied across the saddle of the hammerhead sorrel, and had gone directly to Slim Tymes, the town undertaker and sometime carpenter and substitute barber. Delehanty had shown up almost immediately.

After the marshal had gone through his partner's pockets, finding nothing of any importance, he turned to the Gunsmith. "Like to hear about this more," he said. "Like where you found him, what you was doing out there anyways, and anything else you might have seen."

"Sure," Clint said agreeably. "Have you got an office or do you want to talk here?"

"This town ain't my jurisdiction, and I hear

there is no marshal in Bone City, so more than likely there ain't a office."

"We could mosey over to the Elk," Clint suggested.

The marshal followed him silently out to the street, having first satisfied Slim Tymes that he'd be paid in due course.

"We'll talk, then I got to send a wire to headquarters after I hear you," Delehanty said when they had taken a table along the back wall at Fred "The Marvel" Hooligan's Elk Bar and Good Times Place.

"Who's the law over at Riddle Rock?" Clint asked.

"Dunno. I ain't even sure they got anybody. Likely not. Nearest is Cheyenne, where I'll be sending my wire. Now tell me what you were doing up there and anything else. I know who you are, Adams."

"I figured you did, Marshal. And I sure want to help you any way I can." And Clint proceeded to tell Lije Delehanty all that he thought would be of any use to him in relation to the shooting to death of his partner, Calvin Sutro; leaving out any mention of Conrad or Lorrie Everns and her brother Abel.

When he was through, Delehanty lifted his glass of whiskey. "Cal Sutro was a good man," he said simply.

And the Gunsmith joined him in that.

"And I will get the sonofabitch who done it. Shit, I could've gone with him, excepting Cheyenne said one of us had to stick around here. But I'll get the bastard, or by God, my name ain't Delehanty!"

"You figure Hog Wyatt?" Clint asked quietly.

"Who else?"

But Clint caught something in Delehanty's tone; a hedging. "Well—*who* else?"

The marshal sniffed, his jaw jutted, a long sigh ran through him. "Striker comes to mind," he said.

"Striker?" Clint's eyebrows lifted on that. "Is that Gage Striker, that old-timer? I thought he was dead."

Delehanty looked at the Gunsmith, grave as a tombstone. "Striker is not dead. He has busted out of Laramie, and I wouldn't be surprised if he is on the path." He took a swallow from his glass. "That is why I am here. His old stomping ground. Why Cheyenne told me to stay here instead of sticking with Cal." And his eyes looked off into the middle distance. In a moment he said, "Jesus! It happens one thing and then the pot dumps right on top of you! I never known it to not!"

Clint searched his memory, finding things he had heard over the years—Gage Striker and the Box Canyon Gang. And, yes, Whistler.

"I've got Striker connected with somebody named Whistler," he said. "Wasn't Whistler running some gang and Striker took over; something like that? Back a good piece of time."

The marshal looked at him. He was himself a long man who seemed to be made of rope. Tough. Yet smooth in movement, sharp with his eyes. No man to get on his wrong side. About fifty.

"Yeah. . . ." He leaned back in his chair, nodding into memory, his lips pursed, eyes distant, yet not forgetting where he was.

"Whistler. Aaron Whistler; it was him run the

Box Canyon Gang. And he wasn't your run-of-the-mill owlhooter. Whistler was smart, sharp as a tack, educated. And he could grease that gun of his. Nobody faster. Maybe yourself—that was then." He gave a shrug, leaning forward with elbows on the table, pushing back the brim of his Stetson hat with a rusty-looking forefinger. "He ramrodded the toughest bunch of men you ever seen. Striker, Hog Wyatt—though he was one of the young ones then—the Wagner brothers, Little John Smiles, Roan Kelly, and a few more you wouldn't want to spend any time with."

"But Whistler quit or something like that, didn't he?"

Delehanty nodded. "That he did. He quit. Retired. Turned it all over to Striker; or anyways he likely didn't care who. After he pulled out, Striker took over. But, see, he was different. Whistler was tough, toughest man you'd ever meet up with, but he was fair."

"You knew him?"

"Didn't know him. Not many knew Aaron Whistler. I was around him a couple of times. But now Striker, he was one vicious sonofabitch. Worse than Hog. Hog actually learned from Striker; he was, like, his pupil, if you foller me. Striker shot women, children—anything—old people. He'd shoot his own mother if it suited him. And Hog, he is like that, too. Learned it from Striker. But, see, Whistler was the only one could hold that gang in line. I mind when one time in the saloon—the Ace and Dot it was—when Striker hit one of the girls, and Whistler beat the livin' shit outta him."

"But Striker shot him, is that right?" Clint was

more and more interested in the mysterious Aaron Whistler. He'd heard of him for a number of years. The man was a legend, but before Clint's time. "I hear Striker shot him in the back."

"When Whistler wasn't packing a gun, either," Delehanty said, real sour. He spat at a nearby cuspidor and resumed. "Damnedest thing! I'll never forget it. The marshal got up a posse and caught him, and the townspeople would've lynched the sonofabitch right then and there, exceptin' the marshal stopped 'em. Said Striker was a outlaw, wanted by the law, and he was going to stand trial. And, by God, he did; got put away for life." He spat again, with better aim this time. "But can you beat that! The people—citizens—all riled up to string up a outlaw for shooting and killing another outlaw!"

"Frontier justice," Clint said with a smile. "Sounds like they favored Whistler, liked him."

The marshal nodded. "Yup. I'd say so. Hell, he was a good man; and that's what counts. Counts more sometimes and in some places than what side of the law you're on." He paused, moving the tip of his tongue into a hole in one of his back teeth. "Plenty about the country wearing tin whose ways will sure be questioned when they make it upstairs!" And he pointed toward the sky with his thumb. "Or," he added, "down there!" And he pointed to the floor with his long forefinger.

He took out his sack of tobacco and papers now and began building a smoke. "Funny, Whistler giving up his gang like that."

"Maybe he just wanted to go straight," Clint said. "He sounds like somewhere he was pretty straight."

"But you know, they say you can't never quit—just like that. You, for Chrissake, you know that! Gunfighters, they never quit." He struck a match one-handed on his thumbnail and held it while he spoke around the unlighted cigarette. "How I figure it, Striker was jealous, besides not liking having his ass beaten in front of people like Whistler did over that woman in the Ace and Dot."

They fell silent. The Gunsmith was thinking about Aaron Whistler. Delehanty was thinking about his dinner.

"You'll be sticking around town?" Clint asked as he slipped his hand around his mug of beer.

"I'll see what Cheyenne says." The marshal pushed back his chair and rose. "You?"

"I figure to be here a spell," Clint said. "I'd like to talk to you again sometime," he added.

"Yeah?"

"About Whistler."

"I never knew him. Only seen him a couple of times."

"Know anybody who did know him?"

"Nope." He turned on his heel. He had taken only a few steps toward the swinging doors when he suddenly turned back. "Conrad knew him. Clarence Conrad. I do believe Conrad was the marshal who nailed Striker." He nodded as though agreeing with his memory. "He's got a place up on the North Fork." He stood looking down at the Gunsmith, who was still seated. "It is your business, Adams, but I got a notion there is more to that question of yours than just what you are askin'."

"I'll let you know if it turns out that way, Marshal,'' Clint said pleasantly, and it was plain as the ace of spades he wasn't intending to say another word on the subject, as he stood up and grinned at Lije Delehanty.

Delehanty knew he could have pressed it with his tin star, but he also knew he was taking the right road by letting it rest. He turned away and walked out of the saloon.

Clint wondered how long it would be before Hog Wyatt—or Striker—rode in looking for the second marshal.

The killing of Marshal Cal Sutro stirred nobody in Bone City; the fact that he was a United States deputy marshal added nothing to the event. On the other hand, the fancy escape of Hog Wyatt with his girl friend Honey Hooligan was enticingly delicious the more it was told and embellished. Honey, Clint soon learned, was the recalcitrant, rebellious—not to mention beautiful—daughter of Fred Hooligan, known as Fred the Marvel, who ran the Elk Bar and Good Times Place and was also a power in town.

Prior to Honey's liaison with Hog, she had been married to none other than Horace Harpe, considered the unchallenged number-one citizen of Bone City. Harpe was somewhat older than Honey, yet a man, it was said, with undiminished sexual fever. He was a number of things in the way of business—banker, mining expert and speculator, land agent, and some opined, money-lender who knew how to use a nutcracker.

As far as the Gunsmith could deduce, Harpe held no vengeful feelings toward his former wife or her lover; indeed he had wasted no time in importing someone equally, if not more, beautiful from San Francisco. And Clint had to agree that the woman sharing Harpe's dinner only a few tables away from where he and Lorrie Everns were having their noonday meal was unquestionably a superior specimen of lush womanhood in its prime. Yet the Gunsmith had to admit that while his attention had surely been distracted at the sight of the gorgeous creature with Horace Harpe, his feelings were more engaged with the quieter, softer, more contained girl seated only the distance of his breath away from him. And his attention quickly returned, his pulse beating now in a faster tempo as she smiled at him.

"Yes, she is beautiful, isn't she."

Clint felt himself really caught in surprise at her neat awareness and the way she handled the situation.

"Forgive me. I was rude. But let me say that I wouldn't trade for anything."

Her laughter tinkled across the table. "You talk like a real gentleman, Mr. Adams."

"I must," he insisted. "In the presence of such a lovely lady."

And for a moment she had forgotten her role, he realized, as she returned quickly to her quietness, her seriousness.

"I'm absolutely certain that Abel will come out here; and he may be here already. Of course, he won't realize I'm here." She sighed. "He's a very independent lad and stubborn. Oh, lord, how he is stubborn!"

Clint had decided not to tell her he was planning to ride out to see Conrad; one reason being that he wasn't sure that man was a true lead to anything

regarding her father, and the other was concern
for her, with Hog Wyatt and Striker about.

Nor did he mention Riddle Rock. Lorrie had
said that her brother had left home several days
before she had, and he could very well have gone
to Riddle Rock; indeed, he could easily have been
in Bone City earlier. He rejected the notion of
making inquiries; it would only draw attention to
the boy, the girl, himself, and who knew what
else.

"You seem to be deep in thought," she said
suddenly, with a questioning look in her face.

"I was thinking about you."

"Oh. . . ."

"I was also thinking about your problem. But I
cannot tell a lie; I was thinking that if a man has to
have a problem, he couldn't do better than having
a problem like yourself."

And he watched the wonderful surge of color
coming into her soft cheeks.

He had just parted company with the girl outside the hotel where they'd eaten, when he felt
somebody coming up behind him. Somehow he
almost knew who it was before he turned. He'd
noticed Horace Harpe sizing him up in the hotel
restaurant.

"Mr. Adams, excuse me, but may I introduce
myself? I am Horace Harpe."

Clint offered his hand, the suggestion of a smile
at his lips as he appreciated the oil in the man's
voice; the smooth, unctuous manner in which he
stood there in the street.

"I wonder if you might join me for coffee, or
for that matter, perhaps some stronger libation?"

"I do have a few minutes," Clint said easily. "But perhaps you could let me know what you want to speak to me about."

Harpe let a smile play over his face, as though the two of them were sharing a secret. He was a tall, thin man, with narrow shoulders, eyes set close together, a sharp nose, bronze eyes that were quick and seemed to miss nothing. He was dressed expensively in black broadcloth; he was scrupulously clean; he smelled faintly of pomade, which he must have applied generously to his full head of wavy hair.

"I've a few subjects," he said. "Money. The law and safety of Bone City's citizens, uh— possibly a gentleman named Wyatt, another named Striker. . . . Need I go on, or couldn't we speak more profitably under more appropriate conditions. There's the Silver Dollar across the street."

Clint's appraisal of the man rose as he realized the extent of Harpe's knowledge of a number of people's movements, including, it appeared, his own.

At the Silver Dollar they retired to a back room, the bartender obsequious in the presence of Harpe, and Clint noticed, aware of who the Gunsmith was at the same time.

"Yes," said Harpe when they were seated at a table in their private room with beer at hand. "Yes, they all know the Gunsmith."

"So?"

Clint was beginning to press for action. He realized how Harpe loved to play games, but he was not one to join in. "Why don't you get to the point, Mr. Harpe. You want me for something.

That is to say, you want my gun. Lay it on the table. As I said, I have a few minutes."

Harpe's smile went all the way across his thin face. He leaned forward and lightly slapped the palm of his hand on the baize tabletop. "I like a man who talks straight from the shoulder, Adams. I believe we can do business." With his eyes still directly on the Gunsmith, he lifted his glass of beer and drank.

"There is no law in Bone City. No town marshal, no sheriff with jurisdiction. The town's growing; there are children, a school, old people. You may or may not know, Adams, that Bone City and Riddle Rock are presently at the mercy of whoever carries the fastest gun. Fortunately, we have been lucky. So far." He paused, eyeing Clint carefully.

"You want me to take the job of marshal, that it? You know, you've got at least a temporary lawman in Lije Delehanty."

"Yes—as you say, temporary. But in any case, I was not asking you to be the marshal of anything."

"Oh? What, then?" But Clint already knew the answer.

"I need a man I can trust, a man who can handle a gun, a man who isn't afraid of. . . ." He paused.

"Of Striker or Hog Wyatt," Clint said, filling in.

"Precisely."

"Sorry."

"I will pay you handsomely. Name your price. And. . . ." He held up his hand swiftly before Clint could again turn him down. "And I might possibly be able to steer you and your young lady there at dinner in the direction of her brother."

Clint was once again struck—and more forcibly this time—by the extent of Harpe's knowledge of town affairs. Yet he remembered that, of course, Lorrie had been making inquiries.

"I have my ways of finding out what's going on," Harpe continued. "The young lady, as you know, has been making inquiries around town. But—let me put it this way." He took out a cigar, offering one to Clint, and there was a not unpleasant pause in their conversation while they lit up.

"Pure Havana," Harpe said. "Get 'em sent from Frisco. Fresh. I've sent shipments back that weren't." He grinned.

Clint thought he looked suddenly like a young boy.

"Let me put it like this, Adams. I am not asking you to be my private policeman. No—it's not that. But we need someone to police the town. Yes—a private policeman, but for the whole citizenry. Just until this crisis is past. If we try getting someone from Cheyenne, it will be too late."

"You're sure there is a crisis, then."

"I know there is. Striker is out, and I know he is headed this way. More than likely—I repeat, more than likely—Striker will contact or be contacted by members of his old Box Canyon gang. Hog Wyatt being one. And by the way, you mention Marshal Delehanty. I wouldn't want to be in his shoes. We saw what happened to his partner. We —the people who live in Bone City and Riddle Rock—know the caliber of Hog Wyatt and Gage Striker only too well. Will you take on the job? I appeal to your sense of civic duty. Not only myself, let me add, but others. We've a committee in town, citizens who are concerned about such matters, and we unanimously want you. A private lawman. You don't have to wear a star. You will also have a free hand.''

In the silence that followed, Horace Harpe drew on his cigar. And then, at a certain moment, he spoke again. "Striker will tree this town. He'll kill Clarence Conrad for sending him to the penitentiary when he was marshal, but he'll also wreak his vengeance on the town whose posse ran him down. He has said so. He promised, swore it. You can check if you doubt my word. People here are afraid, Adams.''

"Are you afraid?" Clint asked suddenly.

"Of course!" And Horace Harpe lifted his cigar and took a long drag on it, pluming the smoke toward the ceiling.

Watching him closely, Clint Adams was certain there was a grin hidden behind Harpe's concerned face.

"I'll think it over," he said.

FOUR

"Watch this here!" Gage Striker reached into the pile of cards on the rickety table and pulled out a ten of hearts. He tossed it toward Hog Wyatt. "Nail that on the wall there."

The girl reached for the card.

"Him, I said!"

Striker glared at her out of his bushy face, red flesh showing through some of the gorse that constituted his beard.

When Hog picked up the card the girl said, "Are you his goddam servant?"

"Shut up," Hog said.

"Just so I know I'm living with a couple of gents," Honey snapped. "Christ! I'm going home."

"You're stayin' right here," said Striker. "Exceptin' into the other room with me, that's where you're going to be going!"

Striker had his eyes on Hog as he spoke, his fingers drumming on the tabletop.

"You going to put up with that, Hog?" Honey demanded, her anger fighting with the tears that she could hardly hold back. "Are you going to let me be spoken to like that?"

"Aw, he's just kiddin'. Now take it slow, Honey."

Striker, meanwhile, was shaking with laughter. "Get that card straight. I want to show you two how it's gonna be." He sniffed, then spat on the floor.

"What a gent!" the girl snapped, her mouth twisted in disgust.

"Straighten it!" Striker ordered. "There. Now nail it." He stood up suddenly, the empty keg on which he was sitting falling onto its side and rolling. "Reckon you can hit one of them hearts, Hog? You never was much good at shooting. Exceptin' in somebody's back, of course."

"Gage, lay off me. I ain't gonna take that from you now. That was the old days. I was a kid then. So I learned from you. But I ain't going to put up with that now."

"Come over here and shoot one of those hearts," Striker said, chortling into his wiry beard. "See if you can. Then maybe you can talk like a man!"

Sullenly, his big face dark, Hog stood next to Striker and surveyed the small target.

"Which heart you gonna hit, Hog?" Striker asked, his voice purring with innocence.

"That top right one."

"Go ahead."

Slowly, Hog settled into his stance, as the girl watched the two of them, stilled into fascination with the drama; not wanting any part of it and yet drawn helplessly in her excitement and concern.

Suddenly, Hog's hand dropped to his holstered six-gun. He drew slowly, took careful aim, and fired.

"Try again," Striker said calmly, but he couldn't hide the glee in his voice; not that he even tried.

Hog took careful aim again and pulled the trigger.

"Close, but no cigar!" cried Striker as Hog's bullet nicked the lower corner of the card. "One more chance."

Hog shifted his stance, raised his gun, sighting carefully.

"Make it six," Striker said as Hog missed again. "I don't think you can do it, even with all six."

"Bet I can," snarled Hog and he fired.

"Closer, but still not the one you said. You got two more."

Hog was sweating. "I know I can hit that sonofabitch," he said. And he lifted the gun and fired and missed the card completely. And then he fired again, hitting the card right in the upper right heart where he had said he would.

"There, by God!" He lowered his gun, his face wreathed in triumph. "Now then, let's see what you can do!"

There was a pause, and Hog Wyatt found himself looking right into the cold green eyes of Gage Striker.

"I know what I can do, Hog. I don't need to show you."

"But. . . ."

"But. . . ? Is it? You said you learned from me, Hog. I'd say you didn't learn a damn thing."

"What do you mean? Fer Chrissake, Striker, what's the matter?"

"You are stupid. Plumb stupid. You didn't learn nothin' from old Striker, you dumb shit-head!"

"Gage, c'mon, take your turn."

An appalling silence now fell in the cabin. The girl thought she was going to scream as she watched the two men: Hog with his legs shaking, his face drained of color, his eyes bugging out of his bony head like a couple of eggs; and Striker, something like a snake, fascinating them both with a madness that terrified her.

"My turn is right now, Hog." And Striker drew his gun with a movement so fast neither of them could watch it. Suddenly the big Navy Colt was in his hand.

"You goddam fool, Hog. You learned nothin' from the old days. Nothin'! I got me a full loaded gun. And you—how many you got?" He started to laugh. "How many, Hog? Me—I got six and I need only but one, Hog. And you got none. Shit, man—didn't you learn from old Striker never—never to empty your gun like that!"

"But Striker, we was—we was just playing a game."

"Wrong! You was playing a game, Hog. Me, I never play games. I play for keeps."

"No, Gage. No!" Hog took a step backward, and Striker brought the big gun up and slammed him right across the side of his head.

And as Hog slid down, Striker hit him again. And a third time, pistol-whipping him, while the girl stood there screaming.

Hog Wyatt lay on the floor of the cabin in his own blood.

"Shut up!" Striker said to the girl. "He ain't dead. Just teaching you a lesson," he snarled down at the inert man. "Don't never try to sass me again. Never!" He looked at the girl. "Nor you neither, you bitch."

Honey Holligan felt she was going to be sick to her stomach. But she fought and gained control of herself.

"This is how it's going to be, gal," Striker said. He grinned at her, a great gap showing in his filthy beard. "Now, reckon you better get your boyfriend there cleaned up. We got a lot of planning to do." He holstered his gun, sniffing, clearing his throat. "You mind me," he said. "And we'll all get along. Either of you don't mind me, next time I'll kill him, and maybe you, too. Now cook us up some arbuckle. I ain't had a decent coffee in this good while."

In the brilliant forenoon Clint Adams unsaddled Duke and took off his bridle. He slung the saddle and blanket onto the corral poles outside the town livery and hooked the headstall and bridle over the saddle horn. Duke stood close, nudging him with his nose.

"Want oats, do you?" Clint said. He ran his hand over the big black gelding's back, then felt the soft, velvet nose, warm in his hand. His hand ran down Duke's left foreleg, and he picked up the foot and looked at it.

"Throw a shoe?" said the hostler limping out of the livery.

" 'Bout to," Clint said, studying the hoof.

He dropped Duke's foot and straightened up.

"Reckon I'll have to yank them, else he's liable to go lame on me."

"Take him down to Cy Owens. Cy's the best blacksmith in the country. Don't cost you much, neither," said the hostler, chewing vigorously and spitting with such speed that he never broke his rhythm, or so it seemed to the Gunsmith, who was filled with admiration.

"I think I'll do him myself. Here, if you don't mind it," Clint said.

The hostler was wearing a cap, the peak bent into a greasy V, and every now and again he reached up and tugged at it. He did so now, the gesture suggesting he was emphasizing the power of his position to say yes or no. He chose the former, nodding agreeably to Clint.

"You got yer tools? I see you got yer forge in yer rig back there. Want you to know I bin takin' good care of yer team."

"I know that. Wouldn't have left them here if I'd thought otherwise." Clint grinned amiably at the old man. "I might be staying longer than I thought," he went on.

"Long as yer money's good you can stay long as you like," the hostler said, and then with a hard scratch at his baggy behind he limped off to the livery, every few paces throwing his head back to look at the sky to squint at the weather.

Clint slipped the rope halter onto Duke's head and tied him to the corral post. Then he walked into the barn and checked his team of horses. Next he walked out to the shed at the back of the barn where his gunsmithing wagon stood and fetched his portable forge and shoeing tools. Duke rolled his eyes when he saw the shoeing box, the clippers, the hammer, rasp, and leather apron.

"Easy, big fella. I'm just going to give you a nice new set of shoes. But first, a can of oats."

When he'd given the big horse the oats and talked to him more, he began pulling the shoes. Then he set up his portable forge. He trimmed Duke's left forefoot and filed it flat so the new shoe wouldn't wobble. He liked the smell of the hoof shavings. Then he heated the new shoe in the forge, turning the handle of the blower until the iron was almost white hot. He lifted it out with the tongs and put it in a bucket of water.

Duke rolled his big eyes at the steam and pulled back on his halter. Clint fitted the shoe, making it the right size with his tongs and hammer, burning its outline into the hoof.

He put nails in his mouth so he could reach them easily and began to hammer the shoe on, hooking the nails over quickly after he had driven them through the hoof. He clipped the hooked ends of the nails, then filed the points and buffed the hoof with his rasp so that it fit tight with the shoe.

He held the foot between his legs, facing Duke's rump and leaning against his side as he worked. He laid Duke's rear legs in his lap. Duke stood well, and Clint talked to him as he worked. Most of the time he was working, a black and white mongrel dog sat only a few feet away and watched him. Clint was glad for the company. He was finishing up on the last shoe when he realized he had other company. Only it wasn't a dog.

He had just set down Duke's leg and straight-

ened up when the slightly brisk voice said, "Is it
Mr. Adams?" And he realized the new odor that
he suddenly smelled was perfume.

"That's who it is," he said, turning to face the
woman who had been dining with Horace Harpe
at the hotel restaurant.

She was even better-looking up close, with a
classic figure, finely chiseled features, and a look
in her hazel eyes that was a combination of haugh-
tiness and naughtiness—as Clint defined it to himself. One thing was clear, she smelled of money.
The perfume that braced the air right then had to
come from some place such as Paris or New York.
And the look in her eyes now, which was commanding, had surely been learned through a certain experience with men. All of these impressions
ran through the Gunsmith in a flash as they stood
facing each other.

"What can I do for you, ma'am?"

"I'm Andrea Caudell. While we've not been in-
troduced, I believe we did meet in a rather special
way recently—during luncheon?" And her exquisite eyebrows lifted as she offered the question.

"That is so," Clint said. And he added, just to
bring the conversation down to its heels a little bit,
"Sure enough."

She gave a tickling laugh at that, evidently realizing what he was doing.

"Mr. Harpe, Mr. Horace Harpe," she said, her
tone of voice taking on the quality of an an-
nouncement, "requests the pleasure of your company for dinner this evening; or as it is said in this
country, for supper."

Clint was trying to trace the very slight accent he

heard as she spoke and decided that, possibly, she
was French. Not that it mattered. What mattered
was that she was surely one of the most attractive
women he'd ever encountered. And she kept looking better.

"Why?"

"Why?"

"Yes—why does he want to have dinner with
me?"

"I imagine he wants to get to know you. You'd
have to ask him that."

"I'd like to get to know you better," Clint said.
"And that could be dinner, a walk, a ride, anything."

"Why?" she said, playing it back to him.

"Why?"

"Yes—why?"

"Because I like the cut of your rig."

And they both laughed at that.

"Well, I accept. The only thing I can add to
your proposal is that Horace—Mr. Harpe will be
with us."

A painful grin came into the Gunsmith's face.
"Didn't anybody ever tell you that three is an unnecessary number when two are concerned?"

"Neatly put, sir." And she threw back her head
and laughed. He found her totally delightful.
Then suddenly she was serious. "Will you come?
He does want to talk to you. And you see, I am
—uh—spoken for." And then she turned and
looked toward the livery and the sky, but Clint
was certain he heard the words. "Sort of. . . ."

Of course, Harpe had wanted an answer to his

offer. And Clint had told him that yes, he would take on the job as a temporary "policeman," but only after consulting with Lije Delehanty. He might even consider acting as Delehanty's deputy, but strictly in a limited way.

"And only because of the crisis that you tell me is imminent," he'd added. "I want to check this all out with Delehanty. I'll be riding over to Riddle Rock, likely."

To all of which, Horace Harpe had agreed. The dinner had been amiable. Clint had appeared at Harpe's house about a mile out of Bone City and had enjoyed a royal treatment with servants serving an excellent meal with wine, brandy, cigars —and with the exciting ambiance of Horace Harpe's lady friend. In her evening gown, Andrea looked even more desirable. At one point he caught her smile as she noticed how he was trying to shift in his seat so that he wouldn't be quite so uncomfortable. And later, when he took her hand to say good-night and to thank them both for the evening, he thought he was going to rip his trousers. Especially since he could tell by the look in her eyes that she knew very well what was going on.

And the next day when she appeared at his hotel, he was astonished by his own joy as he experienced simultaneously his surprise and something in him that had known very well that she would come.

"You knew I'd come, didn't you?" she said, as though reading him.

"Of course. And you knew I'd be waiting."

For a few delicious moments they undressed

each other slowly, but then passion engulfed
them, and their last pieces of clothing were torn
from their pulsating bodies.

Then, naked as they stood by his bed, a moment
fell on them of the most exquisite desire that refused to hurry, that, in fact, dictated itself. It
wasn't there for long, for in the next moment he
was burying his face in her upturned, quivering
breasts, putting her nipples in his mouth and sucking, with his erection driving between her wet
thighs, while she reached behind herself to tease
the head of his cock with her fingers.

Then he had her down on her back, but she
slipped down to take him in her mouth, deep into
her throat, and now sucking with long, slow,
soaking sucks until he thought he would go mad.
In the next moment she had released him and with
her legs wide and up high in the air she received
him inside—tight, wet, and driving as she accepted
his rhythm, demanding more as her loins pumped
with his, crying into his ear softly but insistently
with the most exquisite drops of joy as they became one, moving from moments to seconds,
faster and faster and deeper and higher as they
rode each other to the vanishing moment when
neither knew any longer what was happening.

They lay entwined, exhausted in their joy as
their breathing quieted, and the marvelous thrum-
ming spread around their bodies.

"My God, my God," she whispered. "I knew
you'd be good. So good!"

He kissed her ear. "When I looked at you I
knew I would, too," he said softly.

In a little while they began to stir again.

"I want you in my mouth this time," she said.

"So do I." And he rose up, offering his erection to her eager lips.

She kissed the head of his cock, licked it, teased it up and down its great shaft, and then when he could hardly bear it any longer she accepted him hungrily into her starving throat and sucked until he all but choked her in his ocean of come.

After they had lain there awhile she said, "I must go."

"I'd rather you came," he said, smiling into her eyes.

"I was only waiting for you to ask me," she said as he rolled over on top of her.

He didn't enter her though, but moved up toward her breasts as her hand gripped his organ and played its wet head on her nipples. Now with her other hand she teased his balls, until he was almost at the edge of another huge ejaculation, and he drew away and now ran the head of his pulsing cock over her eyes, into her ears, through her hair, teasing it along her quivering lips but denying its entry into her mouth until neither of them could stand it any longer, and he slid down and mounted her, sliding into her wetness and stroking, finding the rhythm instantly and now riding to the moment where neither one was anything other than pure joy.

It had been a while since he'd first thought of visiting Clarence Conrad, and he realized now that he couldn't wait any longer. The morning was fresh as he rode up through the long valley of the Greybull, with the river rushing southward, thick

with still-melting snows and often with debris torn
from the river's banks along the way—great
chunks of uprooted trees and bushes, the freeing
of what was no longer needed in the spring break-
up—as he saw it, nature's cleansing. The sun, the
sky brilliant in its own delight, it seemed. Existing,
which was all that was called for. Now as he rode,
he watched an eagle arcing across the wide valley,
it, too, filled with its life. And for a moment, Clint
Adams thought of the people who had once inhabited this land—the Shoshone, who, like the buffalo, were disappearing. He felt no sentimentality
about this thought. It was the way it was. He knew
Indians. He didn't grieve for what had happened
to them. Those Indians he knew and had known,
the old men who knew how to look at the sky,
wouldn't have wanted anyone to sorrow for them.
It was beyond that. "What is, is," an old chief
had once said to him.

Now, there was the action at hand. To engage
only in what was before you. The Indians, the
mountain men, the trappers, and the old cattle
and sheepmen knew this. And men like Bill
Hickok knew it. You dealt with the immediate.

He wondered how Lije Delehanty was doing.
He had wanted to talk with him again, before seeing Conrad, before making a definite response to
Harpe's offer. But there had been no news on the
marshal, and he had realized he shouldn't wait
any longer.

Now the trail narrowed as it wound through a
thick stand of willows, cottonwoods, and box
elders. He was at the riverbank now and knew he

would soon be crossing the bulging river to take the trail up the mountainside to Conrad's place.

After a while he broke out of the trees and with the river roaring louder in his ears, he approached the wooden bridge. It was sure a rickety affair— triangular pilings built of logs and loaded with rocks for stability, supporting limbed branches and thick boards that made the runway across. Cables were tied to two of the pilings and fastened around trees on each bank. Even so, the whole contraption gave a look of questionable stability. There was no railing and with the louder roar of the river and the splashing of the water coming up onto the bridge, Clint had a job holding Duke down to a walk. The big black was high-stepping, arching his neck and snorting as they clattered over the loose boards. Both of them were glad to make it across.

Now the trail rose almost straight up for about two hundred yards, then veered to the right on an upward angle, then left, following a switchback course, until at last they arrived at an almost flat place where Clint spied a spring box. Stepping down from Duke, he let him drink, and then using the brim of his Stetson hat as a dipper, he drew water for himself. It was pure, fresh from the heart of the spring. Then he mounted up again and rode Duke at a slow walk into the ranch. There was a man coming down from the log house. He was carrying a sawed-off shotgun. Clint could see that his right hand was like a claw. He was an older man, but there was no hesitation in his walk, no backwatering in the stern look of that grizzled countenance, no denying this was a man who'd likely seen it all. He knew it had to be Conrad.

"The name is Adams, Clint Adams," Clint said as he swung down from Duke.

"Conrad," said the man with the shotgun. "That's a hoss you got there, mister."

There was no doubting the sincerity of Conrad's admiration for Duke. Like a lot of people who really appreciated good horseflesh, Conrad wasn't afraid to say so. "What kin I do for you?"

Clint had decided that the best way was to lay it on the line with Conrad, and there hadn't been anything in their meeting to make him change his mind. He told the older man then about Hog Wyatt and his escape, about Lorrie Everns and her brother Abel, and about how he was mixed into the affair, plus Horace Harpe and his offer.

"You're that feller they call the Gunsmith," Conrad said, squinting at him out of his better eye.

"That is what some people call me."

"I'll be calling you Adams," Conrad said. Then he told how he'd already met Abel Everns, and what had happened.

"Where do you think the kid went to now?" Clint asked.

"Dunno. Riddle Rock, maybe. He'll likely run into his sis pretty soon, I'd say."

"What about him running into his Paw?"

Conrad shrugged. "I told you what I told him."

"I've told it to you straight, Conrad," Clint

said. "I've got a strong feeling you know more than you told that kid."

"That is true," the older man said. "But I made a promise."

"The boy'll find out sooner or later."

"Not from me."

"I have got a notion who he was. His father."

"I bet you have. Ain't hard to figure that. But I made my promise. Give it to him when he was dying." Suddenly Conrad looked hard at the Gunsmith. "Listen, it isn't going to be so sweet if Striker learns about that kid looking for his Paw, and maybe the sister, too. You follow me? He can be adding two and two, just like you done."

"I am right with you, Conrad," Clint said with the sinking feeling in his chest and guts.

"Striker is a mean sonofabitch. A mad dog. Nothing stops that man."

"Nothing?"

"Only this." Conrad tapped the barrel of the cut down shotgun with the wide scatter. He added, "And that's what it's going to be." He looked into the distance, then, toward the lowering sun and the rimrocks across the valley. "Striker ought to about be in this country by now. He's had the time now. I'd lay odds he's close."

"You are sure he'll be coming back here."

"He, by God, promised it. He'll be coming back to even it."

"That was a long time ago."

"A man in jail sees time different than others, Adams. Especially a man like Striker. He'll be cutting my trail, you can bet it all on that."

Clint nodded slowly, turning it over in his mind. "Yes, revenge is maybe what kept him going in prison."

Conrad shifted his weight, his eyes going to the mouth of the trail where it disappeared into the trees down by the spring where Clint and his horse had watered.

"Might as well tell you. . . ."

Clint waited during the pause that followed as Conrad brought his thoughts closer. "Can tell you there's something besides just me Striker's coming back for."

At just that moment the door of the cabin opened, and a woman stepped out. "Conrad," she called. "There's a extra place if you've a mind to ask yer visitor to stop awhile."

Without turning around, Conrad waved his arm, evidently in assent, saying to Clint, "Come on up and eat." He nodded toward Duke. "You can put him in the barn, if you like. There's feed."

"What was it you were going to tell me?" Clint asked.

"It can wait." And without a further word, or even a look in his direction, Conrad turned and started walking toward the house.

FIVE

Horace Harpe turned his back on the long mahogany bar, leaned casually on its edge, supported by his elbows, glanced quickly around him, taking in the entire room. It was the main room of Fred "The Marvel" Hooligan's Elk Bar and Good Times Place. The room was large, crowded with men and women drinking, gambling, dancing. Fred the Marvel didn't spare the opulence when it could pay off, Harpe noticed with satisfaction. Indeed, he considered Hooligan a superior arrow in his quiver. Which was why he had married his daughter. The marriage hadn't worked, but then Horace had never expected it to work. He was glad that it had failed, for now, by showing the town that he could rise above it—all the gossip, slander, shady looks—he was actually revealing his clear superiority to the common herd. Horace saw himself as a man well above the mass of men; and indeed he was. There was no question about it, Horace Harpe always and everywhere and inevitably came first. And these days, seeing the development of his master plan filled him with intense pleasure, and at times even awe, for his own talents.

"Lively tonight, Mr. Harpe," the bartender suggested respectfully as he took Harpe's empty glass and replaced it with a full one.

Horace was in good humor. "If you say so."
He pursed his lips, searching for the best words.
"It always appears to be a place for people who
don't want to be where other people want them to
be." And then, "Wouldn't you say?" He had not
looked at the other man as he spoke, but had kept
his eyes on the crowd, speaking over his shoulder.

The bartender didn't know what to say to that,
mostly being unable to follow the play of words,
so he covered himself by moving to another cus-
tomer as though he'd been signaled. Harpe was
sharp enough to catch the maneuver, and it
amused him. Other men's fear of him always
amused him.

His gaze now fell on the wheel of fortune that
was on the back wall, the dice game, the poker
tables crowded with players and spectators. The
room was almost solid with smoke, noise, the
smell of men, and now and then, a trace of perfume from the women, and a shriek of laughter.

Horace had a round, tubular body that showed
no more than his forty years, and he stood well in
it. He suffered from corns and sometimes indi-
gestion and he was losing a little hair, but he was
otherwise fit. He began to watch the faro dealer
setting up his bank only a few feet away. The
dealer was an extraordinarily thin man—short,
looking as though he had only enough strength to
support the derby hat on top of his small head. He
wore a fancy vest over his striped shirt, the sleeves
of which were accented by two bright yellow gar-
ters that looked as though they were too loose.

It was clear, however, that the diminutive man,
whose name was Chip, knew his business. Harpe

could tell. Harpe watched him closely. Harpe was always looking for potential assistants to his scheme.

The man named Chip placed his layout with exacting care: the thirteen-card suit, all spades, painted on a large oilcloth in the shape of a square. The cards were placed in two parallel rows, the ace being on the dealer's left, and the seven, the odd card, on Chip's far right. Enough space was left between the rows for the players to place their bets.

When he was finally set up, Chip shuffled and cut the cards and then placed them faceup in the dealing box.

"Faro bank is open!" Chip called out.

Harpe was considering whether to join the play, for he liked the game. He liked gambling, but considered himself a gambler in a much bigger field than that offered by the Western saloon.

At that moment he felt the presence of a new person standing behind him on the sober side of the bar. But he didn't turn.

"Enjoying it, Horace?"

"It's colorful." Horace Harpe turned to face the portly figure of Fred Hooligan.

They watched each other for a moment, aware that eyes were on them, of course, principally on Horace Harpe.

"How are things," Harpe said, saying the words more as declaration than question, for they were speaking privately in their understanding of well-chosen words.

"Good," the saloonkeeper said. "Things are going well."

Harpe nodded agreeably, and in him was a little song of satisfaction that a certain job had been followed through. Casual though he seemed as he leaned his elbows on the bar, Horace was studying his man closely.

"Want to . . . ?" And Fred the Marvel lifted his eyebrows ever so slightly.

"Happy to hear the family is well, then," Harpe said as a man moved into the slot beside him at the bar. His tone, the angle of his body, his whole bearing indicated that he was declining Marvelous Fred's offer to talk. "Later," he said almost inaudibly, and his eyes moved slightly to his right, indicating where the meeting would take place. His lips had hardly moved; but the other man got the message, and he felt a sudden fear that he had perhaps broken orders. Harpe had made it absolutely clear that they were not to be seen together in public except in casual encounter. Well, the Marvelous One argued with himself, he hadn't actually asked to meet just then, only questioned what was wanted by Harpe and had received the message. So he reasoned furiously as he moved down the bar, but with a little fear licking at him, even so.

Meanwhile, Horace had turned back to the room, sweeping his eyes over two or three of the girls—for later—noting that they were watching him for a sign. It was toward a buxom redhead that his gaze dallied. And the message was given and received in the girl's secret smile.

Yes, he was telling himself as he left the Elk Bar and Good Times Place, maybe the gorgeous Andrea could put that in her pipe and smoke it; having at Adams the Gunsmith of all people! Did the little fool think for a minute he wasn't having her watched! And as he strolled down the street toward his house, he was thinking where else Andrea Caudell could put it.

It was evening when the first knock came on Harpe's door, and Andrea Caudell admitted Fred Hooligan. She showed the visitor to Harpe's office, knocked on the door for him, and departed; the saloonkeeper allowed his eyes to rove over her mobile buttocks as she disappeared. He was jerked back to business rudely, however, by Harpe's impatient voice calling, "Come!"

When they were seated Harpe said, "You've got things under way?"

"I have hired three more men, that brings the total to ten."

"You checked them thoroughly? They are reliable?"

Hooligan nodded. "I check them; they're good men."

"Tell me about them." And Harpe had taken up a pen and a piece of writing paper.

Fred the Marvel bit his lip to control his anger at being treated like a schoolboy. "The Cole brothers, Sid and Mike Cole. They're dead shots, from Texas by way of Abilene. They've been around. And Myles O'Reilly, who used to work for the Stockgrowers' Association. He's a fast gun, not an easy man to backwater."

"I've heard of him. How would you rate these three men with Adams?"

Fred's eyebrows shot up into a series of wrinkles

that stretched along his broad forehead. "The Gunsmith? Shit, Horace, you ever seen Adams in action?"

"Have you?"

"No."

"Then you're talking from hearsay. All right, so maybe one man couldn't, but three. . . . Come on!"

"I guess so." Fred Hooligan scratched his head. "But how come you mention the Gunsmith? I thought you wanted him on our side."

"Just in case, my friend. Just in case." His eyes played coolly over the saloonkeeper's face. "You should know that I never—never trust anyone." He chuckled, his eyes almost closing as he thought of something. "Not even myself. How about that, Fred, my lad! Not even me!"

Suddenly Harpe leaned forward, swift as a cat. "But remember, Fred, remember that I trust you." And the words fell into Fred Hooligan with the force of bullets. Their impact was actually physical, and he felt something grab inside him.

After rather a long pause while he watched Hooligan's discomfort, Harpe said, "What do you hear of Hog Wyatt?"

"Nothing," Hooligan said, glad for a change of subject.

"Nothing from Honey?"

"They must've gotten plumb away."

"What about Striker? What news of him?"

"Only that he's out. But you know that. I have heard nothing else."

"Hooligan, he'll be heading for here."

"That's what I figure, Horace." And Fred the

Marvel had used Harpe's first name once again, as he had long ago received permission from its owner to do; but each time now he was feeling it weaken in him. He had the urge to switch back to "Mr. Harpe," yet he used the first name in an effort to bolster his stance. Somehow he felt that Harpe had set him up when he'd told him some months ago that he could call him "Horace." Fred realized that he was beginning to see deeper into Harpe's character, and he surely didn't like what he was seeing.

"Do you have any idea why Striker would come back to this country?" Harpe said now.

"Only thing I can think of is Conrad. Conrad got him caught and tried, and the word is, Striker promised Conrad he'd come back one day and get him, no matter how long it took. I dunno, Ho. . . ." He had started to say "Horace," but something stopped him.

"Freddie, my boy."

Fred Hooligan couldn't tear his eyes away from those two bronze eyes of Horace Harpe's, which were bulleting him to the wall.

"Freddie . . . you're lying."

Hooligan felt the blood draining away from him. He didn't trust himself to say anything, for he knew if he started, he could end up killing Harpe. Or being killed. For he was sure that there were other men in the house, sure that Harpe had guards around. A man like that never took chances. Never.

"I'm not. . . ." The Marvel felt his voice coming out like water.

Those two bronze eyes were nailed to him as

Harpe spoke. "You know why Striker is coming back. Yes, there is the man Conrad. But you know what other reason. You've known it all along."

Suddenly Harpe stood up. He wasn't a tall man, only average height, and slightly shorter than Hooligan, but every inch of him was right there in his anger. "Don't you ever lie to me again. I am giving you this chance, because—because of Honey and my affection for her. Do you understand, you small thing? If you should even think of lying to me, Hooligan . . . I don't find it necessary to tell you what the consequences would be."

"Mr. Harpe. . . ."

"Stay close to the saloon, that's where you'll pick up any news on Striker, or Wyatt, for that matter."

Horace Harpe sat down at his desk then and began looking at a piece of paper. He didn't move, nor did he speak as his visitor left the room.

He heard the front door open and close and almost at that precise moment the door of his office opened, and he looked up.

"You heard?"

Andrea nodded, smiling as he rose and came around his desk to her.

"Well, what do you think?"

She slipped her arms around his neck. "I think it's time we had some fun."

"I couldn't agree with you more, my dear." And he began to undress her, while her hands dropped down to his crotch.

"In the bedroom?" he said, his breath coming

fast as she reached into his trousers and pulled out his erection.

She didn't answer. She slid down the length of his body to her knees, while his hands cupped her firm breasts; and now she began licking his hard shaft, up and down its entire length, and then bending, taking his balls into her mouth, while her hands played with his rigidity.

Horace could hardly remain standing. His knees buckled, and in the next instant he was on the floor.

"God, God, God . . . Andrea, the door, it's not locked." He was on his back with her straddling him now, both of them half undressed.

Suddenly he moved from beneath her, pulled up her skirt and pulled down her pants. "On your hands and knees," he commanded. He had also pulled off his remaining clothes.

Now he entered her from the rear, driving his organ high into her as she squealed with delight. Now pushing her with his cock, she began to move across the floor on her hands and knees. He directed her to the door, and without missing a stroke, reached up, and locked it.

"Dammit, dammit. . ." she said as he began to explode inside her. "I wanted you to leave it unlocked. . . ."

They had eaten well. Nellie Conrad had cooked up game and hominy grits and rutabagas and baking-powder biscuits. And while Conrad was not a man for talk, Clint had found both Nellie and Nancy Conrad, a lovely child just growing into her teens, to be more than sociable.

Afterward, as he led Duke out of the barn and into the round horse corral, Conrad said to him, " 'preciate your not mentioning what we was talking about before. Don't want to get the women upset. They're already knowing about Striker, but it's good not to bring it out."

"Sure," Clint said, tightening the saddle cinch on his old stock saddle.

"They met the boy, liked him, and wanted me to get him to stay a spell. But that would be a mistake. Striker'll be heading here like a arrow. Well, maybe not like that straight."

"I know what you mean," Clint said. He was standing beside Duke with his hand on the saddle horn, looking at the older man. "You said Striker had another reason for coming back besides wanting to get even with yourself."

Conrad was looking up at the sky. His good hand snugged into the top of his trousers, while he scratched the side of his jaw with the thumb of his game hand.

"That is so," he said. He sniffed and then spat. "You know, Aaron Whistler, he pulled off some pretty big holdups—stages mostly, but he got some gold shipments, too. He was a wizard at organizing. And I bin told it was almost never anything went wrong. Whistler, he figured everything out to the minute. I knew him that well to know it was so. See, before I was with the law, I knew him. That is between you an' me, though I guess it is something some people still about know. Anyhow, not when I knew him, but later, I heard he did some real big hauls. Now maybe it ain't so.

You know how people talk." He paused.

"And people don't know what he did with the loot—that it?" said Clint.

"That's the size of it."

"One of those people being Striker."

Conrad nodded and spat again. He was staring into the distance.

"You're thinking he could be coming back to collect that."

"If he knows where it is he can have it, far as I'm concerned." Conrad spat again. "Thing is, maybe he don't know where it is. People been talking about it on and off this good while, but nobody ever found out where such a cache is. If there is one. And I wouldn't be surprised if Striker didn't know. Whistler wouldn't've told a man like him."

"So if he comes back looking for that, and he doesn't know where it is. . . ." Clint looked carefully at Conrad. "You're thinking he might figure you'd know. Or maybe even your wife or daughter."

Clarence Conrad was silent. He didn't even nod. But Clint knew that was exactly what he was thinking.

" 'Course there is something else, too," Conrad said after a short silence.

"I have been thinking that right along with you," Clint said. "So I'll see if I can run down that kid."

"And the girl, too," Conrad said. "Don't make no mistake about Striker, Adams. Being dead is something a man welcomes if he's on the wrong side of such a man as Striker."

"I gotcha."

The Gunsmith stepped into the stirrup and swung onto Duke, settling comfortably into the saddle.

"Where'll you be headin'?" Conrad asked, squinting up at him.

"Bone City first. See that the girl's all right, then if the boy isn't there I'll go on over to Riddle Rock."

And with a nod at Clarence Conrad, he kicked the big black gelding into a light canter as he headed toward the trail that would take them back to Bone City.

Clint didn't dawdle on the trail, but kept pushing. He didn't need Conrad or anyone else to convince him of the caliber of Gage Striker. Men of such cruelty were not common about the country, but they were not extinct, either. And it was only too obvious that such a man as Striker would think that maybe Whistler had passed on some information to his family. But of course, that meant that he'd have to know that Aaron Whistler had had a family. Clint wasn't going to leave it to chance that Striker wouldn't know. For that matter, he reasoned, there might even be others who knew about Lorrie Everns and her brother. Lorrie, he knew, had been making inquiries around Bone City, and surely Abel had been doing the same at Riddle Rock.

Duke kept up a good pace, and Clint was glad to see the town come into view as they rounded the big butte. There were a number of people in the street as he rode in. Some heads turned in his direction.

It wasn't very long before he heard it. Marshal Lije Delehanty had been shot and killed. The bullet had hit him squarely in the back.

The old hostler filled him in on details.

"Someone high up done it," he said. "Somebody up on a roof. Doc could tell from the angle of the bullet going into the body." He wagged his old head sagely, expectorating, too, as he considered the gravity of his news. "Jesus! That is two lawmen in a short space. Somebody—if it's the same, and there's many thing it was Hog Wyatt the both times—I says, somebody is *invitin'* the law to come to Bone City. 'Course, there mayn't likely be enough marshals to go 'round, neither," he added.

The Gunsmith had stripped Duke and was rubbing him down with sacking. They were in the livery barn, and a couple of the other horses nickered as Clint brought oats for Duke. It was quiet in the barn, away from the town, which he'd felt was agitated when he rode in.

"You be leavin' him long?" the hostler asked as Clint finished up, lifting his saddle up onto the stall rail and laying the bridle over it.

"Can't say," Clint replied, studying the other man now for a moment, for he heard something in his question that was more than ordinary interest or curiosity. "Who wants to know?"

"Just askin'." And the old man hobbled away to avoid any further questioning from the Gunsmith.

Somebody, Clint knew, was definitely interested in his movements. It had come through the

old hostler loud. But who? Harpe was the first
name that came to mind. Yes, very probably
Horace Harpe, who would be still waiting for his
answer to taking on the "private police" job.

Interestingly, it was Harpe who he first ran into
as he crossed the street.

"You've heard the news, Adams?"

"Haven't heard anything but," Clint said. "I
also understand it was a Winchester .44-.40."

"I heard that, too." Harpe nodded.

"Same as shot Sutro."

"It could be the same man." Harpe was smok-
ing a cigar, and its sharp aroma cut into the fine
air, stronger than the usual smell of horse manure
from the street. "I hope you've thought over my
proposition, Adams. We need you more than ever
now."

Somehow his tone of voice caused the Gunsmith
to take a long, second look at him. But Harpe was
simply Harpe, the Harpe, at least, that Clint
Adams had known thus far. He could detect no
guile in the man who said those words. And the
thought passed quickly from him.

"I've thought it over, Harpe. And I'll take a
crack at it. See how it goes. But—we both understand—I will expect a free hand."

Harpe's flushed face bent into a big smile. "But
of course! I wouldn't have it otherwise. We—uh
—wouldn't. I'll be telling the others, and I know
how relieved they'll be. We'll all sleep better now,
I'm sure."

"I would still sleep with one eye open," Clint
said. "Neither Striker nor Hog Wyatt are the kind
of men who ever sleep when they're on the prod."

Harpe gave a chuckle at that, more social than from any real humor. "Thank you for that. I understand very well what you're saying."

The Gunsmith's next stop was at Mrs. Roman's to inquire for Lorrie Everns. And to his good fortune, it was the girl herself who answered the door.

"I'm so glad to see you," she almost blurted out. "I hadn't seen or heard from you in a while, and I began to worry. I've also heard nothing from Abel." She stopped suddenly, blushing just a little, and stepped back from the door. "Oh, forgive me. I'm rude again. Not inviting you in. Please, do come in." And she led him into the parlor.

"Have you any news for me?" she asked quickly as she sat down in a chair facing him.

"On your father, no. I'm going to ride over to Riddle Rock now, after we've finished talking, and see what I can dig up there. But I did talk with someone who met Abel. Clarence Conrad. You remember, you mentioned him."

She was suddenly on the edge of her chair, her eyes lighted up. "Oh, what did he say? Where is Abel?"

"Conrad doesn't know where he is. He might be in Riddle Rock, which is another reason I'll be going there. I think it better if you don't."

Her face fell. "But why not? He's—he's my baby brother. . . ."

Clint's voice was soft as he said, "That's exactly why not. You see, do you?"

"No, I don't understand."

"You called him your baby brother. I think he

wants to be called something else."

"But I never call him that to his face!"

"No. I'm sure you don't, but you have that attitude, and he wouldn't be human if he didn't somehow feel it. Do you see what I mean? I felt this before, your protectiveness. Head of the family, as you put it. I hope I don't offend you."

"Oh, no, no! You don't. I just want him to be all right."

"Then trust me. Will you trust me?"

"Yes." She was biting her bottom lip. "He's all right, is he? The man said?"

"He said Abel looked fine. Kind of like any other cowboy."

She almost smiled then. "Will you tell me—I mean, I know you'll tell me—but soon. As soon as you can."

"I promise you that I'll get news to you—probably in person—just as soon as I know anything. Conrad said that Abel looked very well."

"And what else did Conrad say?"

"Abel stayed for dinner, and then apparently rode back to Riddle Rock. I need to find out more before I can go into it, really. I have a couple of trails I can follow. So please bear with me. Trust me. I'll go into the whole of it next time. Will you trust me?"

She was looking at him with a strained expression on her face, almost as though not knowing whether to believe him, suspecting he was holding back, which of course, he was.

"I'm not going into the whole thing now

because a lot of it is simply guessing. And there would be only foolishness in raising your hopes without any substance. You see what I mean?"

She sighed, her face relaxed, she almost smiled at him. "Yes, yes, I understand. I'm just, well, upset, worried about Abel." She looked down at the back of her hand, which was lying in her lap. "See, I'd thought of going over to Riddle Rock myself, but then I was afraid that when you turned up, we'd miss each other."

Somehow, her remark, which he realized wasn't at all personal, gave him a warm feeling. He smiled at her.

"I've got myself hired on as a sort of special detective or lawman for a man named Horace Harpe and his business associates."

"I see."

"What I'm saying is that, in such a capacity, I hope to find ways and means of finding out something about your brother and your father. But I think I can find Abel in Riddle Rock. That's where I figure he'll be making his headquarters."

"Please, when you see him, tell him I do want to see him and talk to him."

"Of course." And he was relieved at the way she was taking his reticence, his not telling her the whole thing about Clarence Conrad and Aaron Whistler. It wasn't the time for that. It certainly was not the time. In seeing her containment, the way she trusted him, he discovered his feeling for her was even deeper. But at the same time, she had to be protected. If Striker or anyone connected with him should discover that Aaron Whistler's children were in the country, it would not be pleasant; not pleasant at all. It would be a hell of a mess.

She walked him to the door as he took his departure.

"I want to say something." He turned toward her as he spoke. She had her hand on the door latch and had not yet opened the door. "I want you to be careful. There's nothing you should worry about. But this is a rough country out here, and you are an attractive woman who is living alone."

She colored a little then, then said with spirit, "But Mrs. Roman is with me."

He smiled fondly at her. "Good. Stay with her, then."

He turned and she put her hand on his arm. "Clint, I feel there's something you're not telling me."

"Whatever it is I'm not telling you has to be something I don't understand yet, and because I don't see it clearly—whatever the situation was with your father—then I want to be cautious." He smiled at her, looking right into her eyes. "Besides, he might suddenly just turn up."

"Yes," she said. "Yes, he might. But I don't think so." And her face clouded a little.

Clint reached up and put his hand gently on the side of her face. Then he took her chin and lifted it just enough so that he could kiss her on the lips.

"Take care of yourself," he said. When he left her his heart was pounding, and the surge of force in his crotch was almost at the bursting point.

•   •   •

In the box canyon the days were shorter than out on the plain. The sun hit the rimrocks early and shadows began to fill the canyon, while outside in the open land the light was still commanding the sky. Honey Hooligan stood on the broken-down porch of the cabin and watched the light fading on the trees, the grass, the corral that Hog and Striker had put back together after years of disuse. The two men were inside the cabin, playing cards and drinking. She looked at the horses in the corral. Could she make it? Not too likely. She was a good rider, but they would be up and after her in a flash. Yet she continued to plan as she picked up the bundle of laundry and walked to the clothesline and began pinning up the faded, but now clean, clothes.

She wondered how much they would drink. There would come the point where she would be in demand, but afterwards . . . what about afterwards? There was no question about going along with either man's lust. Honey didn't want to get carved up. The only thing was to escape. But how could she prevent them from following immediately? Perhaps if they drank enough. Then would they pass out in their drunkenness? She wondered. She was thinking that Hog would. He slept soundly, she knew. He always had, for she always gave him a good time. Striker was something else. Whatever happened, whether they slept heavily or lightly, she had to escape. Sooner or later they'd beat her again, and maybe even kill her. She knew this. Honey Hooligan was a person who didn't fool herself ever about the ways of the world she lived in. She hadn't fooled herself about Hog.

She'd known what a beast he was, only it was what she'd wanted. At the time. Then. But not now. Now she wanted to get away. She wished she had a gun. She told herself that it had to be tonight. She couldn't wait another night. She could really not endure another night, for she foresaw that their activities with her would only get to be more violent, more disgusting. And as she stood there in the twilight by the clothesline with the heavy wash sagging it almost to the ground, she felt her eyes stinging. And in the next moment, the tears began to trickle down her cheeks.

She brushed them away with the back of her hand, but that gesture seemed only to encourage the flow. In the next moment she was sobbing uncontrollably. As the dark began to fill the box canyon she slipped down to her knees, her whole body shaking with her sobs and she lay down in the grass, bent into a small shape, crying into her hands.

After a while she stopped. She lay there, listening. No sound came from the cabin. But she noticed that the lamp had been lit. Were they still playing cards and drinking? She rose and crept to the window and looked in. They weren't at the table, but then she saw them lying on the floor, apparently asleep.

Swiftly she turned and ran to the corral and pulled down one of the saddles that was on the top rail. The plan that had been growing in her was to hobble the other horses, in order to delay any pursuit, but she saw quickly that this would take too much time, and besides they could slash through the rawhide hobbles in no time.

It took her a few moments to catch one of the horses. She had to move carefully not to spook them, and she was also terrified that either Striker or Hog would awaken. Good fortune was with her. She caught the sorrel gelding, which was the one she wanted. She was good with horses and got her rigging on quickly.

She groundhitched the sorrel and then hesitated. On an impulse she went back to the cabin to take another look through the window. The men were still asleep, lying exactly as before. Maybe she could sneak in and get a gun. Maybe—maybe she should kill them both. No, it was better to get away. She realized that though she wished them both dead, she didn't want to kill them.

It was just as she reached the corral again that she heard a horse approaching, then another. And in the next moment she saw the outlines of the two riders.

"This here's the place," said a man's voice.

Honey froze where she was. But it was too late. They spotted her.

"Striker inside?"

She managed to make her voice steady as she said, "Yes."

"Tell him Roan Kelly's here. And Little John."

SIX

There was a marshal's office in Riddle Rock, but no marshal. Clint Adams noted the lettering on the filthy window as he tied Duke to the hitch rail. A lounger was seated on the stoop outside the feed store next to the former office of the law. An oldster, chewing something or other—maybe tobacco—and breathing rotgut into the clean mountain air. And sniffing through a big nose that was shaped like a sickle.

"They ain't no marshal if that's what yer lookin' for, mister," the lounger said. He wore a battered Stetson hat that looked as though a pack rat had been chewing on it. There was a ragged hole in the crown and cuts along the brim. Clint took him for a busted-up bronc stomper from another day; too old and too beat up to handle any green stuff and more inclined to booze and running his mouth than much else. Ornery, too. He spat indolently at a pile of horse manure in the street and watched the Gunsmith with a glint in his filmy eyes.

"What happened to the marshal and how long has he been gone?" Clint asked.

"Oh—he ain't gone. Marshal's still here." The old bronc-stomper's jaws were chewing fast as a prairie dog's. He'd lifted his head so it was right at the top of his neck, like a rooster. "He is still here—a permanent resident—up in the cemetery," he added. This remark was followed by a cackle.

"That funny remark of yours is pretty old," Clint said. "Now let's cut the gabbing and tell me where a man could throw his duffle for a night."

The oldster was a bit taken aback, but he saw that Clint was friendly and not trying to brace him and he eased back into himself, carefully turning his head as he spat so he wouldn't come near Clint's feet. "Down yonder," he said, and nodded toward the south end of town. "Lazy Marie Boomer. She'll take care of you."

"I am looking for a room, a bed," Clint said.

"That's what I know, mister. I didn't figure you'd be hankerin' after Marie. Hell, if she's a day old, she's got to be a hundred. I mean in the shade."

Clint chuckled to himself as he walked down the street toward Lazy Marie Boomer's Rooming House. Lazy Marie looked to be everything the old bronc-buster had suggested. She was big, fat, with stringy hair, filthy hands, and a leer as she sized the Gunsmith up and down, her eyes lingering at his crotch.

"I am looking for a room for the night," Clint said, feeling decidedly uncomfortable under the landlady's scrutiny.

"By yerself?"

"Right. There isn't anyone with me, and I don't want anyone," he said quickly to pin it down.

She turned on her heel with a wave of her big hand to indicate that he should follow her, saying over her shoulder, "Lemme know if you change your mind, dearie."

With another slow leer she left him in the dingy room, which smelled of camphor and, he thought, sweat and tobacco. But it was all he needed. He didn't linger, but made for the nearest saloon, where under the pretext of making inquiries about Lije Delehanty's killing, he probed for any news on young Abel Everns. And came up with nothing. Nor were any of the other drinking establishments offering news of the young stranger. Finally, at the barber and bath across the street from Lazy Marie's, he struck bonanza.

"Young feller, eh? Mebbe only about sixteen, somethin' thereabouts?" The barber, a man in his fifties who looked like he was all bone and gristle and Irish, went by the name of Hawkins O'Toole. "He was 'ere. I give him a haircut. Nice lad. Didn't catch his name, though. He didn't mention it, for the matter of that. Nor did I ask, being as I am a man who minds his own business. I believe in that. Always have. Me dad taught me that if he ever taught me anything, it was that."

"How long ago?" Clint asked.

"Lemme see. . . ." The bushy eyebrows withdrew to cover the closed eyes as Mr. O'Toole buried himself in a tomb of thought. Almost a minute passed as he stood absolutely still.

Suddenly his eyes sprang open. "It wuz the night Danny Glendinning had the fight down to the Eagle Bar with Barney Gilhooley. I recollect it clear."

"What night was that?"

"That night was. . . ." The eyes withdrew behind the great eyebrows again. Speaking this time with his eyes still closed as he rummaged into memory, the barber said, "The night of the pa-

rade. Yessir, bedad! It was the night of the pa-
rade. Why, I'll never forget that night!''

"And that was . . . ?'' The Gunsmith wondered
if the man was funning him, but he rather thought
not.

Suddenly O'Toole slapped his thigh. "A Thur-
r-rsday. Thur-r-rsday it was,'' he said, rolling the r
through the whole word.

"Yesterday? That was Thursday,'' Clint said.
"You saw him yesterday?''

"No—no, no! Thursday. Let me see, the one
before. Yes, it must have been Thursday a week
ago. I dunno. Something like that.''

Clint gave up. No, O'Toole was like that, he
wasn't spoofing. "Do you have any notion where
I might find him now? Know if he's still in town?''

"I don't know. Why not ask over there where
you're staying, at Lazy Marie's?''

"I already did.''

"Lazy couldn't help you.''

"She said she couldn't.''

The barber was giving him an interesting look at
that moment. He spoke now with his words suddenly sharpened. Gone was his former vagueness.
"You the law, mister? That boy do somethin'?''

"No. I'm just looking for him, for a friend. I
am not the law.''

Hawkins O'Toole's eyes dropped to the Gunsmith's holstered Colt. "I'll take your word on
that, stranger. You want a haircut? Shave?''

"Just the bath. I handle my own razor.''

"Reckon that's about the way to get through
this world,'' Hawkins O'Toole said. "I do the
same.''

Clint picked up some more news at the livery,

where Abel had rented a horse.

"Said he was looking for a place called Kilton, besides old man Conrad's. I never heard of any Kilton. Anyways, I sent him to Conrad's. He come back, but I ain't seen him since."

When Clint asked in the Spade & Heart Saloon about a place called Kilton, nobody had ever heard of it. Then, as he was leaving, a very short man approached him, though for all his small size the gentleman was obviously no one to try to push. He looked to be all muscle. He wore a white beard, thick white hair, and dark eyebrows. Clint could see there was a lot packed into that small frame.

"Would it be Killingtown you're looking for, sir?"

"I don't know," Clint replied, surprised to be accosted by this man who had been standing near him at the bar. "It's for a friend I'm asking, and they said Kilton." It suddenly flashed through his mind that Conrad would have been the man to ask, but it hadn't occurred to him. He'd been too concerned about Striker maybe learning about Lorrie and her brother. And he realized now how the name could have gotten muddled from Killingtown to Kilton.

"What's Killingtown, sir?" he asked. "By the way, my name is Clint Adams."

"The Gunsmith, I know." Instantly the man held up his hand. "Forgive me. I see that you don't care for that monicker. My name is Butler, Harry Butler." He held out a firm hand. "You ask what is Killingtown. Rather one should ask *was*. The town, as far as I know, no longer exists.

It is, quite apparently, dead; inhabited now by pack rats, possibly an occasional deer or elk or even bear, and of course, with not a few of its former residents, now residing well beneath the soil, performing their appointed task of fertilizing nature. I trust the lead in them doesn't retard the process."

"Can you tell me something about the place?"

"It was a town with the hair on, as the saying goes. Nailed together with bullets—a shamble of shacks; that is to say, saloons, a couple of whorehouses, and I allow that's about it. The roost of the Box Canyon gang. You have assuredly heard of same, run by the legendary Aaron Whistler." He paused, moving his mouth about as though searching for some obstruction, a piece of tobacco, a seed. "Whistler, a man who could have succeeded in any field. One hears that lament about such men out here. If only he had chosen a different career! The damn fools who cry this song fail to realize that it is always the career that chooses the man. Eh? How about that, Adams?" And he chuckled hugely at his own sagacity.

"You're saying that Killingtown was the gang's place for fun. They ran it exclusively, I take it."

Harry Butler nodded. "Indeed. And when the gang collapsed, so, of course, did Killingtown. I'm sure that's the place you're looking for. You see how Killingtown could become Kilton."

"I do." Clint smiled at his companion. "And you're saying that's where the Whistler gang holed up."

"Yes, I am." The short man nodded. He was very short, coming only as high as Clint's shoulder. "As I understand it, Killingtown wasn't actually in the same box canyon where the gang headquartered; but some distance away. A little town apart, where they could enjoy themselves, as it were. Except that it was well hidden in amongst a number of further box canyons. That part of the country is riddled with those kinds of hidden canyons. Perfect natural corrals for wild horse wrangling and amazing fortresses for defense against the more determined posses. Whistler, as you may know—or, on the other hand, may not know—was never apprehended by the law. He always escaped. He met his—and I feel I must say, untimely—end at the hands of a disgruntled member of his gang."

"What happened?" Clint asked.

"The sonofabitch shot him in the back."

"But the law got the man who did it, I hear."

"That is so. Rather, Marshal Clarence Conrad got him. And the killer—his name was Striker—was sent away for life. But it appears he has escaped, and everyone supposes he will turn up here to wreak vengeance on Conrad, who now is an old and crippled man, no longer a town marshal." He sighed. "Thus, you have been brought right up to the present. I wish you luck in whatever enterprise you are engaged in. I've heard a lot about you, Mr. Adams. All favorable." And he smiled a big smile, all over his face.

"Maybe you could help me, then," Clint said.

"I am at your service!"

"Tell me how to get to Killingtown."

"Anyone here know how to write?"

Somebody said that one of the Bindels knew, but Sid Bindel said no, he didn't and neither did his twin brother Billy.

"What about the girl?" put in Roan Kelly. "She looks like she's bin to school."

"Not her," Striker said. "I might of broke her hand, anyways, when I hit her and she fell."

"Teach the bitch not to try sneakin' out on us and stealing a horse," Hog cut in savagely, glaring across the cabin at Honey. He could hardly see her through the thick haze of tobacco smoke.

There were a dozen men gathered, with Striker seated at the table, the others squatting, sitting on the floor, or some standing.

"What you want somebody to write for, anyways?" Roan Kelly asked. He was a large, though lean man, very muscular in his tight-fitting shirt and pants, and he fancied himself, with his brace of tied-down guns.

Striker leered across the table at this comment. He didn't like Roan; but then, he didn't like anybody. But Roan was always on the verge of challenging him. He had tried to switch him off onto Hog, but Roan had his aim on the big man. Naturally. This had been going on for the day and a half that the gang had been at the box canyon. But Striker wasn't worried. Striker wasn't the sort of man to worry about such things. He knew he was the best. Hell, hadn't he bested Whistler himself?

"We're gonna do the writing," he said, "on account of we want to keep a record of what we're doing."

"What the hell for?" demanded Little John

Smiles. "Shit, just be tellin' people our business. And it ain't nobody's business but our'n."

"Learned it in Laramie," Striker explained patiently, his eyes on Roan Kelly's sneer. "Newspaper feller came there and wanted to write somethin' about me. Asked me to put something down. Only I took off before I got a chance to do it."

"So you want yer name in the newspaper and with us along with you for the law to see it. For Chrissake!" Roan had taken a step forward, his face flushed with anger.

"Take it easy, Roan," cautioned Little John. "We are here on business. That can come later."

Little John was a lot shorter and smaller all around than Kelly, but Roan listened to him. They'd been partners a long while, and Roan knew Little John Smiles had the brains.

Roan controlled himself, and that was no easy feat.

Striker was staring at Roan, his eyes loaded. "You lookin' for somethin', Roan. Huh?"

"Let's drop it," Roan said, hardly moving his lips, which were on the point of trembling with anger.

The cabin had fallen into total silence.

Striker was holding his big eyes right on Kelly. "I mind the time you shit in yer pants, Kelly, when we was pulling the Willow Creek stage job. You mind that?"

A couple of the men started to laugh but cut it off abruptly. Roan Kelly's eyes were burning.

"You'd like to whipsaw this here, wouldn't you, Roan. I know you. Your kind. Now you mind me, mister, you are not gonna be whipsawin' anything, exceptin' maybe yer whanger when you're hard up.'' Suddenly Striker bent down and came up with a throwing knife he'd had strapped to his leg. ''Hog, you nail up one of them cards on the log there. No, no, we'll do her another way.'' He was leering at Roan Kelly as he stood up and kicked over the barrel he'd been sitting on. He hefted the throwing knife a couple of times, and then swift as a wink he'd drawn it back and shafted it to the log wall where it drove in deep.

''Pull it out, Hog.''

Hog had to exert himself to get the knife out, such was the force of Striker's throw. Meanwhile Striker had walked to the far end of the cabin. He motioned the men to spread out so that he had a clear line to the gash in the big log wall. He looked over at the girl, who was peering in by the door-way to one of the rooms. ''Watch this, girlie!''

Then, swift as water he drew his big Navy Colt and fired a single shot at the wall. The shot echoed around the room, and the silence that fell was louder than any sound.

''Dead center, ain't it,'' Striker said.

''Dead center,'' Hog Wyatt said looking up close.

Striker was looking at Roan Kelly. He held out his hand while with his other he swept the Colt back into its holster. ''Gimme the knife, Hog.''

They watched in awe now as, smooth as the wind, the big man drew back his arm and whipped that Arkansas throwing knife straight as a bullet right into the center of the bullet hole that was in the center of the first knife cut in the thick log wall.

''Think it over, Roan, boy. We are here on

business. I am organizing my old gang with some new ones added. You ever want to step out of line, Roan, boy, remember what you seen here to-night."

Nobody said a word. The only sound came from somebody's breathing, but no one gave a thought as to who that might be. What they had just seen was too great for anything else.

"We will now get down to business," Striker said, and he picked up the empty barrel and sat down on it. While the men settled themselves he looked around, studying each one in turn.

"The meeting will now come to order," he said. "And our first piece of business will be the Riddle Rock stage."

The day had seemed to break earlier than usual, though he realized it may only have seemed so because the night had been so warm. It was warm now as he rode Duke up toward the north fork of the Greybull, branching off before he got level with Conrad's place, and heading deeper and higher into the mountains.

It was about the middle of the forenoon when Clint and Duke rounded the low-cut bank and followed the thin trail up into the timberline. High above, a band of geese sailed across the clear sky. Watching them, his thoughts went to the settlers still swarming all through the West, still taking up land, putting up their soddies and log cabins, measuring off sections of land to grow corn and beans and cutback wheat. The land was changing fast.

Now, walking Duke past blue asters and shining goldenrod, he began to think about Aaron Whistler and his two children. There was the growing fear in him that Harpe or Striker would discover the two Everns and who they really were. Harpe would be the more likely to discover it, for he'd already mentioned Lorrie and the boy to Clint. But Striker, of course, would have his crazy reason to do them harm, wouldn't he?

Harpe? Well, it had occurred to Clint that Harpe might also know about the Whistler cache. But was it all that big? Would it be something that would concern a man like Harpe? Maybe. But Striker—definitely. Besides, there was Striker's revenge. Who knew where that would lead.

He was beginning to wonder how much further he would have to travel when, rounding a bend in the narrow game trail, he spotted a board nailed to a cottonwood tree. There were words formed by bullet holes, not wholly accurate, but Clint was able to decipher the sign. WELL COME - KILL TOWN. POPLATUN 25 . . . LIVING 15 . . . DEAD 11

It was easy enough to tell that the sign had been there some years and that no horse or man had covered the present trail in a good while. Still, there would no doubt be other trails leading into Killingtown. No sensible outlaw would permit only one way into a hideout and the same way out.

The trail was overgrown, and it was also infested with deer flies. Duke spent a lot of time switching his tail and biting down at his chest, and when they stopped momentarily at a creek, kicking at his stomach. Clint, meanwhile, kept brushing the flies away from his face and hands. But at last they broke through the trees and brush and

Killingtown lay before them.

Clearly this was a ghost town, the ramshackle buildings making their last stand against time and the elements.

He had reined Duke, and now man and horse waited at the edge of the trees, studying the town. It looked deserted, but the Gunsmith wasn't all that sure; he had that feeling that always brought him to a state of caution. Suddenly something detached itself from the corner of a building that broke into an alley. It was a deer. But it stopped, stood still, listening to something; and Clint knew it wasn't listening to him or Duke.

A pistol shot rang out from somewhere among the crumbling buildings, and the deer bounded out of sight. A second and third shot swiftly followed, but Clint had no way of pinpointing where the shots were coming from, except that they weren't directed at him, and the shooting was evidently from a single pistol on the far side of a cluster of frame buildings.

"Let's go, boy," he said, lifting his reins and turning Duke back into the trees.

They spent some twenty cautious minutes circling the town until they finally reached a spot Clint had picked where he might be able to see the pistol shooting. All the time they were circling Killingtown, the pistol shots came intermittently from the same area. By now he knew it had to be someone target shooting.

Turning Duke back into the trees again, but staying close to the edge where a sweep of buffalo grass carpeted down to the first buildings, he rode carefully along the game trail until he saw the pistoleer. As he had thought, the man was shooting at a row of tin cans that were placed along the top rail of a fence. But he had stopped now and was reloading.

Clint watched as he closed his six-gun, holstered it, and stepped to an apparently designated distance from his target. Clint could only see the man's back, but it was no one he was familiar with. Judging by his movements, the spring in his step, he had to be young. Then, as he drew awkwardly and fired, missing, Clint knew who it was. Lifting his reins, he kicked Duke forward out of the trees and cantered quickly toward the figure who, not noticing him, was still shooting at his targets.

Only when he'd emptied his gun did he hear the horse coming up behind him. The moment he turned, Clint saw the resemblance to Lorrie. It was in the nose and eyes. He wondered if Aaron Whistler had looked like that. If so, he knew the boy was in trouble. And Lorrie, too.

Reining Duke, Clint stopped only a few feet from the boy, who was looking at him in some surprise.

"Not a likely place to run into somebody, would you say?" Clint began as introduction.

The boy said nothing.

"You must be Abel Everns."

"That's right, I am. Who are you?"

"My name is Clint Adams. I know your sister Lorrie. She's been looking for you, and she's gotten kind of worried."

"Are you looking for me?"

Clint leaned forward in his saddle, leaning lightly on the pommel and horn, looking down at the boy who was squinting against the sun. He liked him. He was firm but not aggressive. He was his own person. Like his sister.

"Not anymore."

"I see."

The boy stood there, looking up at the man on the horse, waiting.

And Clint waited.

"Clint Adams," the boy said suddenly, his face clearing as though in recognition. "I heard your name about, since I've been out here. You're that Gunsmith fellow?" It was put as a question, and Clint found no offense in it. The boy was looking at him with new eyes now.

"That is what some people call me," Clint said, and he stepped down from his saddle. "Why? Does that make a difference to you? Can't I just be your sister's friend—and maybe yours?"

Abel Everns pushed his hat back on his head and scratched his forehead. Then he lifted his hat and settled it further forward on his mop of corn-yellow hair.

"Will you teach me?" he said, and he pointed with his forefinger at the gun at Clint's hip.

Clint felt something clutch at him, then. Somehow he had known this was on Abel's mind. He had almost read the thought, yet he hadn't wanted to accept it.

"Why?" he said.

"On account of you're supposed to be the best."

"So what does that mean?"

"It means I could learn from the best."

"But why do you want to learn how to be a gun-fighter?"

"If I decide to stay out here, I'm going to have

to know something of that. So why not get the whole thing while it's around."

"And if I say no?"

Abel Everns looked evenly at him then. And Clint Adams knew what he was going to say.

"Then I'll have to learn it another way," he said simply.

Abel Everns squinted at the sky, watching the cluster of small clouds scudding toward the horizon. Suddenly he spat, aiming across his horse's withers, but getting some of it on his saddle horn, and the back of his hand.

Riding beside him, now that the trail had widened, Clint Adams smiled to himself at the boy's evident embarrassment.

"It takes practice, young feller," he said.

"I guess it does." Abel reached up and wiped his mouth with the back of his hand, then rubbed his hand down his pant leg. He was riding the same little blue roan he'd rented from the livery in Riddle Creek.

"We'll pull in by that creek yonder," Clint said. "Rest the horses a bit."

He had been watching closely how the boy handled his horse, but he watched covertly, not wanting to make the young man feel awkward. It was clear that Abel Everns was a greener and had a lot to learn. Yet Clint could see that even so, Abel knew something of the groundwork. He had the beginnings of turning into a good hand. He was doing all right. Clint had even started telling him a couple of things as they'd ridden through the morning; but casually, by the way, the way old-timers told things, always leaving room for the listener. It was the way he had been taught.

"I knew an old woman once, in her eighties. I was a kid, about your age—no, younger maybe —anyway, I worked for her husband, doing odd jobs now and again, and one day I found her cutting up firewood out back of her cabin. So I offered to do it for her, being as how I figured that wasn't work for a eighty-year-old woman. 'No, I can do it,' she said. And without stopping her work or even looking at me, she said, 'In this world, young feller, it don't hurt to know everything.' "

The boy grinned at that, and Clint was glad to see him loosen.

"I know I've got a lot to learn," Abel said.

Clint nodded, looking at the top of Duke's head as he switched his ears against a couple of persistent flies. "So do I," he said.

When they dismounted at the creek, Clint instructed the boy to lead his horse right into the water so that the animal could benefit from the movement of the water on its legs. Both men and horses drank. Clint noticed that the boy was watching everything he did with Duke. He liked that.

"That's right," he said, as he loosened and then tightened the saddle cinch on the big black. "You don't always have to ask; it's better to find out. Then you've sort of paid for what you're learning."

"I can ask some questions, though, can't I?"

"Sure. What do you want to know?"

"Did you know my father?"

"I don't believe so. Anyhow, I don't know anyone by the name Everns."

"He could have had a different name. He was around here, like I said."

They had talked a bit about Abel's reason for coming West during their morning ride. But the Gunsmith hadn't been very helpful.

Now the boy said, "I believe that man Conrad knows more than he is telling me."

"I think you'd better talk to your sister, Abel."

"Sure, I plan to. But I think I want to go see that Conrad again."

When Clint saw Abel looking at him questioningly he knew he had to say something. "Good enough. But be careful not to push anything that doesn't need pushing."

"But I need to find out. Sis does, too."

"I know. But tell Conrad what you feel; I mean, your feeling that he's not telling you all he knows. Maybe he just isn't sure or something."

"It makes me feel maybe my Dad did something wrong, bad. You know what I mean?"

Clint nodded. "Go talk to Conrad," he said. "But first—your sister." He checked himself from again saying that Lorrie was worried about him, but said, "She needs you. It's time you began to take care of her."

He could see in the way the boy looked at him that this was a thought that had not occurred to him.

The trail had started to narrow, so Clint kicked Duke into a light canter as they approached a stand of box elders, cutting in ahead of Abel and the blue roan. For some time they rode in silence, following the dim trail through the trees and brush until they came out into a meadow.

"Horses been here," the boy observed, pulling up beside Clint, who had stopped to scan the near horizon of trees on the other side of the meadow.

"How can you tell?" the Gunsmith asked.

"Horse droppings—over there. Didn't you see it?"

"I saw it," Clint said. "And there, and yonder, too," he added. "Tell me, you see anything about the rider? Say, that one you saw over there."

"I don't know," Abel said after a pause. "I don't see how I could figure anything about his rider from a pile of horse shit."

"You can tell that horse didn't have a rider," Clint said. And when the boy looked puzzled, he said, "A rider never lets his horse stop to crap. Oh, maybe a rare time. But in general it's an unsaddled animal that'll take that time for himself. Now take a look there." He pointed as he drew rein. "How do you read those prints?"

Abel swung down from the roan and walked over to the hoof prints that Clint had indicated in the soft ground. After a long moment he scratched his head. "Only thing I notice is this right forefoot is deeper sunk than the other three."

"Did he carry a rider?"

"Dunno."

Clint had stepped down from the black gelding and now squatted beside Abel. "He was shod, so he had a rider, more than likely. And it looks like he's going lame in that right forefoot. He was moving fast, though. See how the print is torn here." He moved forward without rising, remaining in his squat position. "See there, the same. Heading—yonder." He rose slowly.

"Aren't they pointing back the way we come from?" Abel asked. His blue eyes were alight with excitement. "How come we didn't see anybody?"

"Those tracks are a day or two old; probably two. So we wouldn't have seen them. Thing is, that horse was heading more or less toward Killingtown." He moved toward Duke, who was cropping the sweet grass. "But there were no signs around there, and I did look."

"What does that mean?"

Clint swung up into his saddle. He waited while Abel mounted. "Use his mane to help you get up," he said. "I mean really wrap it like this." And he showed him, wrapping Duke's mane and the reins in his fist. Then he said, returning to Abel's question, "What's it mean? It means there's something out near Killingtown that Mister Horsebacker was in a helluva hurry to get to."

The sun was burning straight down on top of them as they left the meadow.

SEVEN

"Tell me, Freddie, who is the young woman staying at Sofia Roman's?" Horace Harpe brought the question out even before Fred Hooligan had seated himself in the chair in front of his desk.

For an instant Fred the Marvel looked puzzled, fearful, cautious; he let his breath out in a sigh. "I dunno," he said, finally more at ease with himself. Harpe had been pressing him lately, ever since he hadn't been open with him about Striker. "I don't know," he repeated.

"She's been asking questions about Bone City, Riddle Rock, and—Killingtown." Harpe spread his hands, stood up, holding all ten fingers out, his palms facing Hooligan as he came around the desk and sat in a chair closer to his visitor. "And there is some young kid who rode up to see Conrad recently. You know anything about that?"

"Nothing. Horace. . . ." And with a pluck of pleasure, Fred Hooligan realized he had regained some of his courage as he called Harpe by his first name. "I must say you sure have your lines of communication working."

"How else can a man run his business if he doesn't know what's going on, Freddie?" He paused to say Hooligan's name softly, knowing how Hooligan disliked being called "Freddie." "I

102

know just about everything that takes place in
Bone City and a lot of what happens at Riddle
Rock. And we spoke last time you were here about
Striker's reasons for returning to this part of the
country."

"To revenge himself on Clarence Conrad."

"And . . . ?" Like an imperious schoolteacher,
Horace Harpe lifted his eyebrows, his chin, and
his right forefinger.

"And the possible loot of Aaron Whistler."

"The hidden cache, which nobody seems to
know the whereabouts of! Bad English, my
friend, but I am sure you and I understand one
another."

"Thing is," Hooligan said easily now, "thing
is, I don't see how there could be all that much. I
mean, no question that Whistler was one of the
most successful road agents we've ever had
around, but hell, it's no gold mine. I'll bet on
that."

"I think he put a lot of money away. Not
millions, but some thousands, I'd say." Harpe
nodded, agreeing with himself. "Not a sum to be
sneezed at." He raised his forefinger again, his
bronze eyes gleaming at Hooligan. "Remember,
he was an intelligent man, Whistler. You know
how he duped those fools who posted a ten-
thousand-dollar reward for him. You know the
kind of sense of humor he had."

"I have heard something about how he turned
himself in, and collected his own reward."

Harpe chuckled, but more in admiration than
humor. "He just walked into the governor's office
one day holding the reward notice and said,

"Here, I'm collecting it."

"And what happened?"

"He turned himself in, let them arrest him. But they had to give him the money. There was a loophole in the law. That's why I'm saying he was so smart."

"But they arrested him and put him in the pen."

"And—as anyone with half a brain could have foreseen—the prisoner escaped. But with the ten thousand." Harpe paused, savoring the story more as he got into it. His eyes fell fully onto Fred the Marvel now. "That ten thousand could be part—I say part—of the cache."

Hooligan was excited now. He leaned forward. "I never thought of it being all that big."

"Yes, you did, Freddie."

And Fred Hooligan felt a stab of fear lace his guts. "And there could be even more than that," he said, in an effort to recover lost ground.

"Could be." Harpe shrugged.

There was a short silence while Horace Harpe lighted a cigar. Then, blowing smoke almost into Hooligan's face he said, "Would you like one?"

"Yeah, thanks."

"On the desk there. Take one."

Another silence as Harpe waited patiently for Hooligan to light up.

"Where do you suppose Striker is?" Harpe took a drag on his cigar, then removed it from his lips and, holding it a short way from him, turned it so that he could inspect the ash.

"Figure he might head for his old hideout, or I mean Whistler's."

"Up by Killingtown."

"I'd go with that."

"Except that it's one thing to find Killingtown, but something a helluva lot different to find the hideout—I mean find anything!—in that maze of box canyons."

"That is sure," Hooligan agreed. "I know men have got lost in there—lawmen—and just disappeared."

"Still, somebody must know the way in and the way out."

"Old-timers," Fred the Marvel said. "A man like Conrad. He'd likely know. 'Course Striker, and likely Hog, too. You know Conrad rode with Whistler way back—'least that's what I heard —before he turned lawman. They were always good friends, I heard. Could be that's how come Whistler was so lucky."

"Lucky?" Harpe chuckled and drew on his cigar with a thoughtful look on his face. "There is no such thing as luck, Freddie. There is the man who can think, who has good sense, and the nerve to carry a thing through. No, it is not—never is—luck!" Harpe tapped the ash off his cigar and then said, "Does the name Everns mean anything to you?" The bronze eyes waited while Fred the Marvel searched his memory.

"No. Never heard it."

"A while back maybe. Did you ever know or hear of a man named Everns?"

Fred Hooligan shook his head. "No, I never."

Horace Harpe sighed and said nothing further. He sighed again as he let his visitor out and returned to his desk. He was satisfied that in this case Hooligan was telling the truth. It was the main purpose of the meeting to find that out about the name Everns. It had taken a bit of doing to pummel, cajole, to carrot, and whip Fred Hooligan so that in spite of himself the truth could pop out of him, and he thought it had worked. Yes, it had worked. He was sure Hooligan had never heard the name Everns. But he, Horace Harpe could hear it pounding in his head. It was crazy, illogical, it made no sense, but it was also not impossible. Because why would someone have come out from the East in search of a man named Andy Everns! It was a wild thought, a mad thought. But life, Horace Harpe knew, was full of wildness and madness.

He was in a beautiful mood when the door opened, and Andrea walked in.

"Am I on time? I thought I heard your visitor leaving."

"My dear, what would you have done had he still been here?"

"The question is what would you have done, Horace?" And her eyes dropped to his trousers where his erection was at its fullest rigidity, driving against his pant leg.

They were both laughing as he approached her, his eyes poring over her body. Andrea didn't have a stitch of clothing on.

"Delightful," murmured Harpe. "Not a stitch of clothing. Naked as the day she was born."

"But shaped somewhat differently, I trust."

Horace Harpe's erection offered the best testimony to that as he bore her to the floor and mounted her.

• • •

The rider had served well, arriving on a nearly foundered horse, himself lathered with excitement as he brought news of what was aboard the Bone City stage. It was just the news Striker had been waiting for.

And high time, too, he was thinking. The men he had gathered were restless, and it wouldn't take much to set off trouble. Better for them to get their nuts off holding up the stage than having at each other. Even he, he reflected, picking his teeth casually as he watched the group gathered in the cabin. He would have liked to throw down on that sonofabitch Roan right now; excepting he had need of the man.

"This'll be our practice one," he said, leaning forward on the rickety table. "And then one, maybe two, more."

"And then?" It was Little John Smiles bringing the question.

"And then—there is the railroad."

"The railroad!" A gasp or two, some muttering shot through the group of a dozen men.

"I'll be wanting the best from you men. Roan will handle the falling back—to cover us."

"Shit," Roan said.

"Roan . . ." Striker's single word fell like a bullet into the group. Not a one of them, not even Roan or Hog would question the threat in the tone that carried Roan Kelly's name.

"And Hog, you'll stick by me. I will have my eye on you, boy!" His eyes were on Hog Wyatt as he spoke and all could see how amused he was at Hog's reaction to being treated like a greener. It was the way Striker kept authority—through ridicule, threat, and bribery. "Roan will cover us. Hog will see that there be fresh horses at Spring Fork. Dusty will be waiting there with them. Anybody got any questions he can say it now. So you speak up or shut up—one."

Nobody decided to avail himself of the offer to speak up, and so a silence maintained itself for several moments in the crowded room.

Suddenly Striker raised his voice. "You got coffee, hey!" His big eyes swung through the room to land on Honey Hooligan, who was standing in the doorway to the kitchen.

"There is coffee," she said. "For some. For the rest there is bear piss."

Several men let out a roar of appreciation at this sassy remark, the loudest being Striker. "By God, there is a woman with balls!"

"You could use a pair yourself, you big shit!" And she stood there, firm as a whip, glaring at the man at the table, while the room fell into a graveyard silence. The group wasn't sure how their leader would take this, which had gone well beyond just funning.

"If you was my gal—and I ain't sayin' you ain't—I'd surely wash your dirty mouth out with soap," Striker said slowly, turning his eyes onto Hog. " 'Course that is something that will have to wait till we get our business done. Now!" And he slammed the palm of his hand down onto the tabletop. "You get that ass of yours moving, by God, and get us men coffee. And right now!"

She had been standing in the doorway with her hands shoved into her pants pockets, glaring defiance. Striker's words seemed to fall off her as she waited without answering or moving. It was a long moment.

"Honey . . ." It was Hog. "Don't be a damn fool."

With a shrug the girl—still sneering at Striker, who was looking at her hard—turned and disappeared into the kitchen.

In another moment she was back with a pot of steaming coffee that apparently had been keeping warm on the stove. The group opened to allow her passage to where Striker was sitting. Without looking at him she put the pot down, turned, and said to the assemblage, "There are mugs in the kitchen. Get them yourselves."

No one said anything as she walked out the door of the cabin.

After a moment while the men were getting mugs, Striker said, "That gal is too good for you, Hog. I think she needs a man."

"She is my woman, Gage." Hog stood his ground, to everyone's amazement. But it was also evident he was only just managing. He was pale suddenly, and his grip on his mug of coffee required both hands.

A chuckle came bouncing out of Striker's big chest and throat and hit right at Hog. "We'll see about that. Maybe some of you young turkeys needs yourselfs a lesson or two on what makes a man." He nodded his head to a gray headed man at the back of the room. "Eh, File? File remembers the old days. Shit, Hog, you was a kid then, but you shoulda learnt somethin' fer Chrissakes! But you didn't."

The room was silent again. They were used to these observations by their leader, and they had learned not to dispute them.

In the silence that now fell, somebody belched.

"We'll ride, then," Striker said. "And remember one thing." He stood with his thumbs hooked into his wide belt. "I don't want any of you greeners fucking up." And he added, "Not any you old bastards, neither. On account of whoever might—I am sayin' might—fuck up has got me to answer to." His glare ran all around the cabin, holding each one for a moment, then moving on until he sniffed, reached down, and scratched his crotch.

"Let's hit leather!"

Sofia Roman, huge, redoubtable, sympathetic, immediately found room for Abel in her small house and large heart; all but sweeping him to her copious bosom with her combing eyes. Widowed and childless, her behavior didn't appear as strange to the Gunsmith, but he could quite understand why Abel Everns had that guarded look on his face.

In the late evening, the three of them sat in the parlor of Mrs. Roman's house while that lady herself had gone to visit a sick friend. It didn't take long for Lorrie and her young brother to compare notes and come up with nothing.

Conrad, of course, was the one thing Abel had to offer, but the old man hadn't given much—in fact, nothing—of value. Abel's suspicions that he knew more than he was telling were taking over.

"I still feel he is holding back something," he said again.

"But can you be sure," Clint pointed out, knowing very well that Conrad had indeed been holding back, and in a way agreeing with him.

"I feel it," the boy insisted. "I can't prove anything. Just something in his way, his attitude. And then—"

"And then what?" Lorrie asked quickly, bending forward in her chair.

"Mrs. Conrad. I could tell, I felt she wanted to say something. Only she didn't."

"Or maybe couldn't?" put in Lorrie. "Maybe she did have something to say, you're suggesting, but then perhaps Mr. Conrad told her not to?"

He nodded. "Yeah. I think something like that. It was a real strong feeling I had."

"Do you think he might have known Dad then?"

"I don't know. Perhaps something about him?" He turned his puzzled face toward Clint, who was listening carefully to the two of them.

"Could it be he knows somebody or used to know someone who knew Dad?" Lorrie suggested.

Suddenly Abel gave an elaborate and comical shrug, and his two companions laughed.

Clint had simply been listening as the conversation progressed and the two Everns relaxed more in each other's company, glad to be together again and sharing fully their mutual concern over Andy Everns, their father. It was rewarding to Clint to see how they were with each other. At the same time he was careful not to interfere.

He sympathized fully with Conrad's position. The man had given his word to his dying friend. No small affair that. But there was also the prob-

lem of Striker should the outlaw happen to learn
that Aaron Whistler's children were about. Striker
just might want to wreak even further revenge.
But then it had to be only a matter of time—and
short time at that—before the two Everns
discovered who their father was.

Heading back to his hotel room later, Clint
knew that his next move had to be toward Clarence Conrad.

But the Gunsmith was to discover that his next
move wasn't going to be toward Clarence Conrad
at all. As he approached the door of his room,
coming down the long corridor, he caught the familiar smell of her expensive perfume. And he was
instantly erect.

But he didn't let passion dim his caution. He
knew it could be a trap. Andrea Caudell was not
the sort of woman a man could trust. And the
Gunsmith knew that like he knew the back of his
own hand. Silently, he tried the door of the room
next to his, and fortunately it was not locked. He
slipped in quickly, his gun drawn in case anyone
was there. But the room was empty. He crossed to
the window. Locked and there was no balcony, no
way anyone could climb up or down from the roof
to either this room or the one next door. He
waited, listening at the wall but no sound came
from his room. He could still smell her perfume.
He waited a little longer and then stepped outside
into the corridor, listened at his own door, but still
didn't enter. Instead he went back downstairs.

The boy at the desk looked surprised. There was
no one in the lobby, even though the night was still
young.

"How come you didn't tell me I had a visitor," Clint demanded in a no-nonsense tone, holding the boy firmly with his eyes.

The boy, probably twenty, flushed and touched the side of his jaw in a nervous gesture.

"Thought you'd be happy about it, Mr. Adams. The lady said she wanted to surprise you. Said it was your birthday."

"She give you money?"

He nodded.

"Let me see."

Reaching into his pants pocket the clerk drew out a tightly folded ten-dollar bill.

"I ought to take that from you, except it would put me in the wrong kind of business," Clint said.

"Yes, sir."

"Is the restaurant still open?"

"Yes, sir. It's still open." There was the edge of relief appearing in the youngster's cheeks now. "I hope I didn't do wrong, Mr. Adams."

"No, son. You didn't do wrong." And he nodded and turned away from the desk and walked across the lobby and into the restaurant. A cup of coffee would hit well now, and maybe some of that apple pie he'd seen the last time he was here.

His decision had been a good one, he discovered. He enjoyed both coffee and pie. He was just finishing when he caught the perfume again, and she was standing beside him.

"No longer interested?" she said, with a teasing smile. "I heard you outside the door."

"I know. I made sure you did."

"May I sit down?"

He was already standing and offering the seat across from him. "Coffee? Pie?"

"Just coffee. I think that will do nicely."

She was completely at ease and this intrigued him. At the same time, he'd found out what he wanted. It hadn't been a set up; she was on the square with him. At least, a voice inside him said, more or less. He still didn't trust her, but he had to admit he was more than glad to see her.

"Seriously, Clint, I do hope you aren't angry at me for just inviting myself into your bedroom." Her doelike eyes were brimming with innocence.

Clint had thought he was immune to blandishments that were so obvious, but he realized—and happily—that he had been wrong. He found her delicious as now both of them leaned onto the table and poured themselves into each other's eyes.

"For somebody who appears to be quite strongly connected to somebody else you appear to exercise a good amount of freedom," Clint said, watching her closely.

"One must take what one can get in this world," she replied; and he watched as she bit lightly on her lower lip, the edges of her front teeth very white.

He had a quick vision of her getting her way with the young man at the desk, not only with the ten dollars, and taking pleasure at her ability. It was her arrogance that he didn't like, but then as the lady had said, "You take what you can get in this world."

And shortly, in his room upstairs, he did take all he could get and give . . . while the bedsprings twanged, and their hungry bodies pumped each other into delirium.

• • •

He was an older man now and he was tired. It wasn't the same without Nellie and Nan around. But he'd insisted on their leaving, sending them to Jovil to stay with Nellie's sister and husband. Insisted. It was the closest they'd ever come to fighting, but fortunately the moment had passed; and the two of them had departed.

"He'll be coming here," he'd told them. "It won't help me none with the two of you about."

"But why don't you get help?" Nellie had wanted to know, her small face tense with worry and growing anger.

"From who? There ain't no lawman anymore in either Bone or Riddle Rock."

"What about that man who was here, Clint Adams?" she'd wanted to know. "I heard Cy Owens call him the Gunsmith—that time he come out to visit with Emily—and I took that to mean he was likely handy that way. He sure looked like a good man when I seen him here with that big black horse." She gave a sort of a smile suddenly. "He sure eats like a man who knows what he's doing," she said with a wry appreciation in her voice.

"I dunno," Conrad had answered her. "Maybe. But even so, you two got to get to town and over to Jovil."

He was sitting in the kitchen as these thoughts ran through his mind, now looking up at the ceiling of the cabin, now letting his eyes go to the window. Near him on the table stood a cup of coffee.

He didn't feel bad sitting here doing nothing. It felt good. He could just let his tiredness circulate through his whole body. Yes, even his thoughts were tired. He looked at the curtain hanging limp in the window with the afternoon sunlight reflecting on it. Well, he'd ride fence tomorrow on the north side of his place, check his stock. He was running about 250 head, but Nan wouldn't be there to help him now. Idly, he thought how he could have hired the boy.

This thought took him to Aaron Whistler. Long time. And that sonofabitch Striker. Maybe Striker wouldn't come back. Maybe he'd tamed some in the pen. No, he knew better. There was, after all, the cache. He had often wondered himself where Aaron might have hid it. Should be a nice sum in that bundle or box or whatever it was. Aaron hadn't been one to blow his money like most road agents. He had his fun, for sure, but then he socked it away, too.

Well, by God, it was a gut old Striker would be sniffing about for that cache. There'd been a lot of talk at the time Aaron was shot, about the money he'd stolen. And where it might be.

That damn fool, Striker, thinking he could come back like that, like it was the old days. Henry Vails had gotten the word to Conrad right the moment, it seemed, that Striker busted out. Shit, they'd be sending marshals. Though look what had happened to them two that were taking Hog Wyatt in. He sighed. The country now, it sure was changing. And fast. It for sure wasn't what it used to be. Not men about like Aaron Whistler.

And yet, sometimes—like now—it all came alive again. Yes, like it was yesterday. It was that clear. Like that time—down to Killingtown. That time they'd ridden in, hard and hot, and were all having drinks at the Sagebrush; the general store, saloon, dance hall, and anything else you wanted to name it—yes, and whorehouse—by God. They'd just pulled the job on the Lander Stage. But there'd been plenty of lead thrown. Morgan had been hit in the arm, and Tom Hanks had bullets in him in both legs, and he could remember how Big Tom's face had been soaked with pain —his mouth had been bleeding as he bit down against the driving torture in his legs.

Aaron had been creased along the thigh, nothing serious, yet Conrad remembered how he'd thought it must have been painful. But Whistler said nothing, didn't even cuss.

Thoughtfully, Aaron had them bring along a sawbones as they passed by Lander. This was a puffy little man smelling of flour and sweat. Fear sweat. He'd been terrified. He'd wrung his hands—they were thin and bony, he wasn't a young doc—and told Aaron he would do his best for Tom Hanks.

Aaron Whistler was a big man, bigger even than Striker and the others who were pretty filled out, and he stood over that little sawbones, hard, like a rock, with his high, Indian-looking cheekbones flaming with what he had to say. "I don't want your best, Doc," he'd said, and his words cut right into the older man. "I expect Tom here to live long and hearty with both of his legs working under him."

Doc had pulled himself together then, ordered water to be boiled, and soon had got those bullets out and had Tom under bandage and plenty of booze. Tom had passed out. Then Doc tended to Morgan's arm and last, Aaron's thigh. They'd left Tom lying up on the bar, afraid to move him.

Then Aaron had said, "You tell on this and I will kill you." He had said it real easy-like. Like he was paring a fingernail with his big knife. Conrad remembered that, after all these years, that it was that casual, easy way Aaron spoke at times that made him so scary. There was no bravado, there was simple fact. You do this or you'll end up that.

And that sawbones had said, "That's what I know, Mr. Whistler."

"What's your charge for this?"

Doc's puffy white face widened in surprise. "Charge? No charge, Mr. Whistler. I don't charge you, sir." He suddenly scratched himself vigorously under his arm, as though to appear easy in that desperate company. Or maybe, Conrad reflected now for the first time after all these years, maybe that old sawbones just did have an itch in his armpit. And he felt like chuckling at that thought.

But Aaron hadn't taken that answer. He'd stood real big in front of that medical man, saying, "I asked you a question, and I want an answer. Man does his work he's best paid for it. That is, if he's worth a good or a bad goddam."

Then some of the boys had busted right out laughing at the doc's discomfort; him not knowing which way to go.

But Whistler told them to shut up. "Reckon you want your life more'n you want money, that it?" Aaron had canted his head at the older man then, the way he had of doing.

"I guess I do."

"You're scared."

"I am scared."

It was then Conrad saw something about that sawbones and about Aaron Whistler, too.

"Just remember to stay scared," Aaron had said. "There is nothing wrong about being scared. It is the smart thing at certain times. Remember that. Like this time here." He had run his big forefinger along the side of his jaw then, like he sometimes did when he'd decided something. "Here," he said and he handed the doctor money. Then, throwing a look at Conrad, "You take him back."

One of the special times Conrad always remembered. He never saw that sawbones again, but he never forgot him and the way Aaron Whistler had treated him and what he himself had learned.

Then, while Tom Hanks slept on the bar in the Sagebrush, the boys had at the booze, the girls, and just their own high spirits at pulling off another big job.

Long ago. Killingtown. Everyone saying how it had no law and never would have. And now—a ghost town. Only thing left was memories. Until now. Until Striker. Striker bringing back the past. Only there was no Aaron Whistler for that coyote sonofabitch to shoot in the back. But there was himself. There was Clarence Conrad. Now retired. But then marshal of Bone City and Riddle Rock, who'd taken on that office at the time Aaron quit the owlhoot trail. He remembered how Aaron had told him of his plans to leave the country, start a new life someplace else. But he never made it. Thanks to Gage Striker. Yes, he must have been thinking of his family back East then, not that Conrad or anyone else knew anything about that. But the boy and girl were evidence; right now before his eyes.

Suddenly he sat up real straight in his chair as a thought hit him. He got to his feet and walked outside. The sun was just down at the rimrocks across the wide valley of the Greybull, and the whole basin of land and sky was bathed in gold.

By God, he was thinking, by God, that bastard Striker was coming back for revenge, was he! Well, by God, there would be revenge done. He, Conrad would see to it. Revenge for Aaron. And as he started toward the barn and the room he'd built there for his gunsmithing and leather work, he realized finally what it was that had been bothering him for so long. He hadn't known yet what it was in him that had already decided what he was to do. And he felt good. He felt clean and strong all at once and all inside himself as his step quickened.

He was going to kill that sonofabitch.

EIGHT

"One must always take into account the unexpected and the ridiculous," Horace Harpe was saying as he leaned back in his chair, lifting his glass of whiskey to his lips, his eyes on Clint Adams.

They were in Fred Hooligan's place, in one of the back rooms Harpe used as an occasional office or for meetings.

"They got clean away with a tidy bundle of money," Clint said. "Would some of that bundle be yours, Harpe?"

"That is correct." Harpe leaned forward now. "I know—and I'm sure you know—it was Striker. Jerry Miller, the driver, and Hal Burton, who was riding shotgun, tell me they're certain it was Striker, and likely Roan Kelly and Hog Wyatt as well. Nobody was actually seen, recognized, you understand, but Miller and Burton are old-timers; the kind that know horses and men. Both of them remember something of the old days when Whistler and his boys were around, and listen to this, it's interesting. . . ." He held up a long forefinger in emphasis. "Both of them said it felt like it was that old gang. Just felt like it! They pulled the job in the same way—on an upgrade when the team had to slow to a walk, a narrow place in the road with cover on both sides. The same routine:

passengers out, throw down the box, fill the hat. I don't know, maybe it's crazy, but those old boys swore it was Striker. They remember him from long ago.''

"Interesting," the Gunsmith said, taking a pull at his drink as Harpe nodded in agreement.

"Interesting and amusing," Harpe said. "And clever. Now let me tell you a story. You know Whistler was a gentleman. Some folks called him the Gentleman Highwayman, something like that. Anyway, he was always courteous to the ladies, gave them back personal jewelry, all that. Well, you know he once pulled a stage holdup four times in the same place in succession. And get this; this is the touch I like. The leader of the gang—it had to be Whistler—recognized the driver on one of the stages—fellow named Chamberlain who he'd robbed earlier. And bedamned if he didn't apologize for taking Chamberlain's watch with them the time before. Said he didn't have it with him right then, but he'd give it back the next time they met up!''

They were both chuckling hugely as Harpe finished his story about the unique Aaron Whistler.

"That man had a sense of humor as well as knowing right and wrong," Clint said laughing outright now. "But Striker's another kettle of fish.''

"Indeed he is. But he really wanted to be like Whistler, I think. That's what's so damned interesting. He was deeply influenced by Whistler. And while he learned a lot from him and was jealous and hated the man enough to kill him, there was this secret admiration apparently. I've heard stories of how he, too, would be polite to his holdup victims, and so on. But of course, with a heavy, heavy hand!"

"And that's how those two fellows figured it had to be Striker this time."

"It makes sense, doesn't it?"

"I'd say so," Clint had his eyes carefully on Harpe now as he said quietly, "So what's all this to do with me? What is it you want, Harpe?"

A careful smile spread over Harpe's face as he took in the Gunsmith's words.

Clint Adams waited. He knew very well that Harpe had quite simply been trying to create an atmosphere for what he wanted. From the point of view of what was important in his life, he couldn't give a damn what sort of man Aaron Whistler had been. But Harpe had gone to a lot of trouble to make a point, to fix a background for what he wanted. The man was damned clever. No question.

"What do I want?" Harpe repeated the Gunsmith's question from his own point of view, as he drummed his fingers on the table. "I want a peaceful town. I am sure Striker is running a few holdups—oh, I know he'll pull maybe a couple more, at the least—getting the boys limber and in line. Disciplined. His teacher was a disciplinarian. Then he'll go after the big game."

"Which is?"

"Why Aaron Whistler's cache, and not so by-the-way, the rubbing out of former U. S. Marshal Clarence Conrad. This holdup and others, which I bet will follow, will, of course, also serve as diversionary tactics."

"You're suggesting there could be others looking for this supposed booty; not only Striker."

Harpe nodded. "I'm sure of it. Whistler's cache is part of the folklore around here; you might say it's authentic history to some, let me tell you."

"And you want me to find it first."

A slow whistle, hardly just more than a breath, came out of Horace Harpe's lips as he stared at the Gunsmith. "I have always appreciated men who are sharp, Adams. I does save a lot of time."

"It can save lives, too," Clint said, thinking of Lorrie and Abel Everns.

"And," added Harpe, "it is worth money. To me it is worth money. I would pay well for the success of such an enterprise, Adams." He reached for the amber-colored bottle that stood between them. "Have another?"

The Gunsmith pushed his glass forward, and Harpe continued to speak. "You see, when that cache is found, it means something will be out of circulation as it were. There will then be no reason for Striker and his gang to hang around these parts. The road agenting isn't as good as it used to be. They'll soon see it will be better elsewhere."

"You seem to have inside information, Harpe. You know how much is in the cache?"

"I don't know for sure; but I've been given to understand by the most reliable sources that there are several payrolls in there." He began ticking off his fingers. "It is virtually known that the big Wells Fargo express job is there, the Dayton bank job, and the gold shipment from Aurora on the Billings stage, and more." He barked out a short laugh. "I feel sure you can pull it off, Adams."

He leaned forward onto the table, hunching his shoulders. "Are you game? Will you do it?"

And when a long moment passed without Clint saying anything, Harpe asked again, "Will you do it?"

"I will think it over."

And without touching the drink Harpe had poured him, he stood up.

"What you really want is for me to kill Striker, isn't it, Harpe."

"That may be necessary, yes," Harpe said, rising to his feet as Clint walked to the door. "It will save lives by bringing peace again to Bone City and to Riddle Creek. I don't know if you realize how agitated the two towns have become in the past few days. Everyone is aware of Striker's presence and the old Box Canyon gang. I personally wish to allay such fears." He paused as the Gunsmith opened the door. "Please think it over and let me know as soon as possible what you will do. And—uh—Adams. . . ."

Clint turned and looked at Harpe, who was still standing on the other side of the round table, with his fingertips touching the edge of the green baize top.

Harpe's voice was softly penetrating now as he said, "I forgot to tell you that I made some investigations, sent some wires and so on . . . I won't bother you with details, but I feel sure you will realize that when the situation here and at Riddle Rock has cooled down, uh, your friends the Everns will perhaps be more at ease in the knowledge that their, uh, relative or friend, or whoever it is they're so interested in was simply

another good, solid, ordinary citizen doing his
best—but that he remains a mystery, an unknown.
And sleeping dogs will have been left in peace."

The Gunsmith simply nodded and walked
through the door, leaving it open behind him.

Three days later the second holdup took place
along the same route. And again the driver and
guard claimed the Box Canyon gang, risen from
the dead under the iron and vengeful hand of
Striker, was the culprit. Further testimony to this
was borne by the fact that one of the road agents
had dropped a brooch at the scene of the holdup;
the brooch having been taken from a passenger on
the previous robbery.

Clearly, Clint Adams decided, the bandits
wanted to be known. And when later the same day
he conferred with Horace Harpe, he found the
same thought being voiced.

"And so, does this visit mean you'll be working
with me, Adams? I do hope so."

Clint had ridden out to Harpe's house in the
early morning on Duke, and his host had offered
him breakfast. They were now having coffee
together in Harpe's office, or as he usually called
it, his study.

Clint accepted the cigar Harpe offered him and
lighted it. It was an excellent Havana. "I'll look
for the cache. I don't guarantee to find it, and I
sure don't promise to kill Striker. I am not a hired
gun; never have been or will be. Other than that,
I'll see this thing through."

Harpe was nodding quickly even before he
finished what he had to say. "Of course, but of

course! I was hasty there—about Striker. I don't want unnecessary bloodshed. I want to locate that cache and return the money to its rightful owners. Of course, some of that will be to myself."

Harpe reached for his cup of coffee, obviously pleased with the way things were turning out. And he said so. "I must say, Adams, that it is a great relief to me to have you, as it were, on our side."

"Your . . . side?"

"The side of law and order. Justice. Mind you, any assistance in the way of men or money, or whatever else I can give you, just say the word."

"Good enough, then," Clint said, getting to his feet.

"You have a plan? I shan't ask you what it is," Harpe said amiably as he walked him to the front door. "Just remember, the sooner this affair is concluded the better. And . . . there will be a bonus in it for you."

As he pointed the big black gelding toward town, Clint was thinking of Striker. Would the outlaw pull another robbery or two, or would he now take his next step toward finding the Whistler cache? The next step was obvious. The next step had to be Conrad.

He knew Conrad was prepared for such an event. He also knew that Striker wouldn't kill Conrad until he had found out the location of the cache. So there would be the matter of torture. His thoughts flinched at such a possibility. But there was no question that Striker would enjoy the opportunity to torture such a victim.

But what truly bothered Clint Adams was what Harpe had said in their previous meeting; his men-

tion of Lorrie and Abel Everns. The man had ears
and eyes everywhere it seemed. And power and the
knowledge of how to use it. Clint had contacted
Lorrie right after that meeting and warned her not
to talk to anyone. She'd told him she hadn't, with
the exception of Mrs. Roman; though she had in-
quired about the town, asking if anyone had heard
of the name Andy Everns. With Mrs. Roman
she'd been a little more open. It was clear to Clint
that that large, round lady was another example of
the Harpe web and its dreadful possibilities.

Once again he turned Duke's steps toward the
Sofia Roman house, while the thought occurred to
him that the lady might have given her information quite unwittingly to Harpe or one of his men.

He was just inside the limits of the town when
he saw Lorrie walking down the streeet. Evidently
she had been shopping, for she was carrying some
bundles. There was no sign of Abel, and he supposed he might be out practicing somewhere with
his gun. The boy had not broached the subject
with him again, having swiftly caught the Gunsmith's drift. Yet, Clint knew very well how determined the lad was.

The moment the girl saw him her face lit up,
and he felt his own doing the same.

"I'd been wondering what had happened to
you," she said, shifting her bundles.

"Let me pack some of that," he said, reaching
down from his saddle. "I've been about. Have
you any time right now?"

"Oh, yes."

They were soon at her house, and he dismounted and hitched Duke to a nearby railing.

When they were seated once again in the Roman parlor he said, "I think I'm closer to finding out something about your father. I know that still sounds vague, but the whole situation is vague."

"It's rather like somebody doesn't want us to find him," she said. "That's what I've been thinking lately."

"Maybe it's your father who doesn't want it. Have you thought of that?"

"Yes, I have." Her face saddened as she spoke, and she dropped her eyes. Then, brightening a little, "You know, if—when—we find him, or at least find out something about him, what has happened to him. . . . Then if it comes that he doesn't want us. . . . I speak for myself . . . I'd go, I wouldn't insist. I think Abel might feel that way, too. I—I know I would respect his privacy."

"I know you would," Clint said gently. "But I want you to be careful. Like I told you before, don't speak to anyone now about looking for your father. As I said, I think I might be getting close to something, and I'm not sure just what will come of it, so I want to go very carefully."

"Oh, do you really think you might know something soon?"

"I can't say. But I don't want to get your hopes up unless there's really good reason."

"I'm so grateful, Clint."

"How is Abel?"

"Abel is gone again. I don't know if he went out to see Mr. Conrad, or what. I have decided firmly not to worry about him. He's no longer a young boy, but a grown man!" And she looked at him severely as she said that, so severely, in fact, that they both broke into laughter.

Conrad awakened quickly, as he always did.
And the first thing he remembered was they
weren't there, remembering it even before he
opened his eyes, even before the realization that he
wasn't in the double bed, but on the floor of the
front room with the buffalo robes over him. Even
so, he lay there for a moment or two, as he had
ever since they'd left.

At length he got up and stood tall and bony in
his long woolen underwear, scratching himself,
yawning the sleep away, rubbing the slight stiff-
ness in his arms. I'm getting old, he thought. He
stood looking at the wall of the log cabin.

The logs were smooth and straight, and they
smelled good. They had been cut green when the
sap was high in them, peeled with a draw knife,
and left to season. He ran his rough, callused palm
over the smooth surface of a log, remembering
again the summer he and Aaron had built the
house.

"Ach," he muttered, and began pulling on his
clothes. Then he walked out to the kitchen and
built the fire for his breakfast. While the stove was
heating he started on his chores.

When he went out the kitchen door, the black
and white shepherd dog came from where he had
been sleeping under the porch and whimpered at
him, his bushy tail wagging slowly.

It was dawn. The sun was throwing its light all
over the sky and the snowcapped mountains as it
rose from behind the great gray rimrocks across
the valley. And he remembered again how he and
Aaron had built the barn. Aaron had done it for

his family. He'd said how he was going to quit the
owlhoot trail and send for his wife and children.
After he'd been murdered, Conrad had taken the
place. He knew Aaron would have wanted that.

This morning after he'd had breakfast he saddled his buckskin pony and rode out to check his
stock. Not a big herd, but he was holding his own.
It was a good life there, with Nellie and Nan, or it
had been. Now. . . . Hell a man had to do what he
had to do. He didn't get back to the outfit till
noon.

As he rode down the draw toward the cabin he
saw the blue roan grazing and the boy sitting on
the top rail of the corral with a twig in his mouth.

"Well, boy, what kin I do for you?" Conrad
had swung down from the buckskin and now
stood with his hand up on the saddle horn, looking directly at Abel Everns.

"I wanted to ask you about the place I mentioned before—Kilton. A man in town said maybe
it was Killingtown or something like that. But he
didn't know where it was or how to get there.
Anyhow, I found it. It was like a ghost town.
Couple of others I asked never even heard of the
place."

"Then how you figure I'd be likely?" Conrad
asked, his eyes covering the boy's face.

"Figured you'd been around this country a bit-
like," Abel said.

"I told you what I knowed already, son. There
ain't no sense trying to get more out of a dry rag."

The boy stood his ground, facing the man
squarely. "I figured maybe you were protecting
something, thought maybe it wouldn't be something nice for me to know. Like that. I wasn't

doubting your word, mister. Only I felt maybe,
too, that you might have remembered something
you'd forgotten, I mean, since you saw me last,
and I might have stirred your memory about my
dad. I mean, if you ever heard of him or might
know of anyone who could of heard of him.''

Conrad looked toward the house. He was glad
the women had left. For sure they'd have been
into it some way or other if they'd been around.

"Can't help you, boy," he said, starting to strip
the buckskin. "Best thing you can do is head back
for town. You know it'll take you a good while,
the light goes in the mountains pretty early."

He could feel the boy's agitation as he started
toward the barn leading the buckskin.

"There isn't anything in that place but a bunch
of old falling-down shacks. How come it's like
that? I mean, didn't people used to live there?
Why isn't anybody living there now?"

Conrad had reached the door of the barn and
stopped and turned to face the boy.

"I dunno. Likely people got old and died, and
some went away."

"Were you ever there?" And then he stopped,
realizing he'd maybe gone too far. He stood looking at the man with wide eyes.

"I was there," Conrad said. "Used to be sort of
a line camp for some cow waddies and such. Had
a saloon, a general store, smithy, like that. Not
much to shake a stick at. What'd you find there
besides deer flies and snakes?"

"Nothin'."

Conrad had led the buckskin into the barn and
tied him in a stall and was looking for some sacking to rub him down.

"Mister Conrad, if I go straight up that trail back of your house and follow around those high rocks will that take me to Killingtown?"

Conrad had found the sacking he was looking for and had started toward the buckskin. He stopped and faced the boy. "Thought you said you'd been there already."

"I rode in from a different direction. I'm not sure coming at it from this way."

The man turned toward the horse, nodding. "Reckon if you follow that way you'll find it." He turned back to face Abel suddenly. "Why? Why you want to go there?"

"I dunno. I just do."

Conrad didn't say anything to that. He turned back to the buckskin and started rubbing him down. After a while, and without looking around, he knew the boy had gone. And when he went outside, Abel Everns was nowhere in sight.

In the Spade & Heart it was the old bronc stomper who started it. The same boozer with whom Clint Adams had come close to crossing words when he'd first ridden into Riddle Rock not so long ago. The old boy, well into his whiskey this evening, though too old to fork a bronc any longer, was still man enough to hold up the edge of a bar.

He'd just been telling about the new herd of cattle that had been driven up from Texas, 500 longhorns so trail-toughened they were practically jerked beef on the hoof, and who the hell did those drovers think was going to pay for that kind of meat!

But it was the road agenting stories that really held the old boy's audience, and not so incidentally, kept his glass filled. That old fellow had the Spade & Heart crowd in thrall as he related the latest in the growing legend of Striker's new Box Canyon gang. Like people everywhere, the denizens of Riddle Rock loved to hear the stories they knew already. And the revival of the road agents, while inconvenient for a number of persons—Wells Fargo, the railroad, the stage company, and assorted men of business such as Horace Harpe, over whom tears were not shed—filled the saloons and cribs with customers and money and gingery tales.

"The guards is all startin' to git the jitters," the old waddie was telling them. His name was Pony Wagner, and he must have been on the other side of seventy, but spry. He was real spry. "They has got the jitters so bad, the drivers and guards, that some of them up and quit."

"Who quit?" some doubting Thomas, clearly liquored, had the nerve to ask.

"Bo Billings, by God, for one," snapped Pony, and he clicked his teeth together in emphasis, his jaws bulging under the impact like a prairie dog packing extra food. "And Pete Coles. But you ain't heard the latest. . . ." A minor master of drama, Pony paused at the crucial moment to take on more fuel. He overdid it and fell into a fit of coughing. The town barber, Hawkins O'Toole, standing beside him, slammed him generously on his bony back, nearly knocking him to his knees, but the coughing attack stopped.

With his eyes glassy and filled with tears, Pony

continued. "Willie Hinds, that new feller they hired 'bout last month, him and his partner— Clem Fiddle, riding shotgun—was comin' up the long grade other side of Chinese Butte, and they see a feller by the roadside carryin' his rifle and, by God, what'd they do but throw the damn box down at him, hollerin' 'Here's yer damn box,' and Willie whipped up his hosses, and they took off like a cat with turpentine up his ass!"

Pony paused once again for refreshment and also to string out the exquisite moment with himself the center of action. "Thing was, this feller the box was throwed at wasn't no road agent at all. He was a hunter—feller named Wilkins, a English feller, one of them lords I reckon—and a few hours later he turns up at the depot with the box. He'd got a ride with some wagon hauling lumber!"

This marvelous tale brought the entire room almost to the floor with hilarity and amazement. And it also earned Pony Wagner another round.

"Howdy there, mister," the old boy said when Clint pushed up to the bar and ordered a beer. "Howdy. You got yerself all fixed up with Lazy Marie, eh?" And he winked one eye hugely, his wrinkled lid covering his great eyeball like a vulture's.

"I don't know if I should thank you for that room," Clint said, friendly. "That old lady snores through three walls."

This brought another round of laughter from the nearby customers.

"Lazy Marie—I hear tell, mind you, I ain't never sampled the goods—but I hear tell"—Pony,

winding up was almost spluttering the words—"I
hear Lazy Marie always smokes that big black
cigar of hers when she's doin' it."

"Jesus!" somebody said. "That old bird is over
a hundred, I'd bet a month's pay on it!"

Clint, laughing along with the crowd, suddenly
spotted Abel Everns as he walked through the
swinging doors. He waved him over to where he
was standing next to Pony Wagner and his claque.

"What's your pleasure, young man?"

"Beer."

Abel moved in on the far side of Clint, away
from Pony; another man having moved to give
him room.

"I just was talking to Lorrie not long ago,"
Clint said. "What have you been doing? I had a
feeling she wanted to talk to you."

"I took a ride up to see Conrad again. But, boy,
that man is close-mouthed. He says fewer words
than a tree stump."

"He's a man of few words, and he uses them
few damn seldom," Clint said with a laugh.
"That's what they used to say about Texas John
Slaughter. I don't guess he's changed any."

"Who was he?"

"Sheriff down in Tombstone. Toughest man
you'd ever want to meet, and one of the nicest,
providing you weren't throwing too wide a loop."

"I wanted to take another look-see at Killingtown," Abel said. "But I changed my mind."

"Why? What did you figure you'd find out
there?"

"Nothing I guess. Only I'm sure that's where
the name Kilton came from, getting changed or

mixed up in the telling, likely. But what that means I don't know." He leaned on the bar and looked down at the mahogany, moving his glass in some beer that had spilled. "I guess I just didn't know where to look," he said despondently.

"If you don't find out anything about your dad, it won't make the end of the world," Clint pointed out. "I'm only saying that," he added quickly, "so you won't be too disappointed if you and Lorrie don't find anything."

"Yeah, I know."

"See, the West is a funny place. It's all the time moving. People come, people go. It's not settled like back East, where things are more stable. I think that's why people want to come out here. It's exciting."

"That's for sure," the boy said, with a shy grin. He was looking over at one of the girls at a nearby table.

Clint had just caught the look she was giving Abel when, like a crash of thunder and lightning, the man she was with reached over and grabbed her arm and twisted it so that she cried out.

"You little bitch, you stop that! You're with me!"

Before Clint could stop him, Abel had leaped forward, grabbed the man by the shoulder and spun him around. He was a big man, bigger than Abel, and Clint could see by the way his gun was tied down he was not a man to mess with. But Abel was into it now, and it would have been wrong for him to interfere.

"Well, sonny, you want me to dry yer ears for you!"

"Leave her alone!" Abel said. His hand had not moved toward his gun, and Clint realized he was acting in terms of a possible fistfight.

Obviously the big man got that idea, too, and suddenly hit Abel right in the face with a smashing blow of his fist. The boy staggered back, blood streaming from his nose. A circle had cleared around the fighters with the more cautious customers seeking cover toward the rear.

Clint remained where he was, moving his stance just enough so that he could take in the whole room and assuring himself that there was nobody behind him.

Abel had been staggered by the tremendous blow, but he had remained on his feet, to the surprise of his opponent. The boy moved in now, with his hands up, and the two circled each other, their eyes sharp for any untoward movement. Now voices in the crowd muttered encouragement to one or the other battler, but mostly to the older man.

Suddenly the big man charged, throwing a tremendous right hand punch at Abel's head. The boy ducked and smashed the other man in the pit of his stomach. The crowd roared as the big man dropped to the floor, his face deathly white, clutching his stomach in pain.

"C'mon, Roan. Get up and teach the little bastard a lesson!" somebody shouted.

"Don't let that greener get away with that shit, Kelly!"

But Roan Kelly had been hurt. He had received Abel's punch right in the solar plexus. And now he suddenly started to vomit.

"Get him, Roan," somebody hissed from the edge of the circle.

"You had enough?" Abel said as he took a step forward.

The big man had started to struggle to his feet, his right hand feeling for his gun that was still strapped to his side. But he didn't draw. He was only making sure it was still there.

"Kid, don't you know who you're messing with?" It was Hawkins O'Toole. "Why don't you get out of here while the getting's good."

"I'm not afraid of him," Abel said.

"That's Roan Kelly, boy," somebody said.

Clint recognized the voice of Harry Butler, the man he'd talked to a while back, asking how to get to Killingtown.

"And I am Abel Everns," the boy said.

Roan Kelly had recovered now. He was waiting, regaining himself. Clint could see what was going through his mind. The man was fixing to go for his gun.

"Abel." Clint Adams' voice cut into the room clear as a silver dollar dropping into the moment of silence that had followed Abel's words.

"Stay out of it, mister." It was Roan Kelly now, and his voice was as calm as his gun hand, which had moved into position for a draw.

"Abel, leave it. He is figuring to draw on you. And you can't beat him."

"I am not afraid of him," Abel said, and Clint remembered his sister saying how stubborn he was.

"This is no time to be stubborn. The man's a killer. Wait till you've had some practice at least."

"If he'll take that gun off I'll whip the sonofabitch's ass!" The words burst from the boy at the same time that the onlookers began quickly to move out of the way.

"You stay out of this, Adams!" snarled Roan Kelly. "It ain't your fight. Stay out of it. I'll take you after I'm through with him!"

Quicker than a man could scratch himself—as old Pony Wagner was to tell it later—Roan Kelly's hand swept to the big hogleg at his hip. Abel didn't have a chance; Roan's gun had already cleared its holster. But quicker still, and no one really saw it, yet they heard the gunshot, they saw Roan's big gun fly out of his hand. And then their astonishment took in the calm man at the bar, the one known as the Gunsmith, holstering his Navy Colt. Roan Kelly stood there, his face drained of color, his mouth open, his hand, which hadn't been touched by Clint's bullet, numb from the power that had knocked loose his weapon.

"Jesus Christ," somebody whispered as awe took over the entire room.

And indeed, as Harry Butler was later to observe, it was surely the moment for recognition of the deity.

NINE

"I tell ya, the sonofabitch was faster'n Hickok, fer Chrissake!"

The words came tumbling out of the garrulous mouth of a man named Dutch Bellows. "I never seen nothin' like it in my whole entire life!"

"Shit, there wasn't, and ain't, nobody faster'n Wild Bill," somebody said as Dutch whipped a gob of spittle in the general direction of the cabin floor before racing on.

"You wasn't there, Shorty, so go fuck yerself," Dutch snapped back like a feisty rooster. "I am telling you how it was. That Gunsmith feller is so goddam fast it takes two men to watch him draw and shoot!"

While most of the group had fallen into a moment of awe at Dutch's report on the shooting at the Spade & Heart, their leader, on the contrary, had fallen into a long, soft, rhythmic chuckle.

"Where the hell is Roan now?" Striker asked, his voice still graveled with laughter. "I'd sure like to've seen his face when that man shot his gun right out of his fucking hand!" And he could barely finish the sentence as an enormous, wet, choking laugh shook him almost off the upended keg on which he was sitting.

There were some half-dozen men gathered in the cabin, drinking and celebrating the successful robbery of their third stage coach. As with the other two robberies, this one had gone like a clock. The boys were happy, proud of their work, especially pleased that after the long absence they were working with a "tough sonofabitch" like Striker; though necessarily the descriptive phrase of their leader was not uttered in his presence. Newer members, who numbered roughly half, were also pleased to ride with true professionals. As in any business enterprise, the professional was not only rare but much sought after.

Not all of the gang were present; a number, including Roan Kelly, had ridden in to Riddle Rock for further celebration. Striker had not forbidden it; he knew they needed to let off steam, but he wisely kept some of the men back. No sense in showing the whole gang to the townspeople; somebody might get ideas.

Striker felt the little song singing inside him; happy that Kelly had stepped into it. That stupid sonofabitch! Maybe that Gunsmith feller took some of the wind out of his goddam brag. Damn fool was always singing a brag on something or other; usually his fast gun. Fast gun! Well, well!

At the same time, Striker needed Kelly, as he needed Hog and the other veterans. And now he needed Conrad. He had first thought the boys could capture those two women of his; break the sonofabitch like that, get the location of Whistler's big haul. But with the news that the women had gone, he saw the only way now was to take Conrad himself. Good he had restrained himself from killing the man. Which he'd planned for all those years in the lockup. Later, when he'd gotten what he wanted. Then. Maybe he'd let Hog go to work on him first. Maybe like he had on that feller that time he'd shot him all up, keeping him alive and then at the end of a whole day of it, finally killing him. And, by God, cutting off his ears to boot!

"Hog!" the word bounced out of him suddenly, even surprising himself, the speed with which it had followed his thought.

Hog was at the other side of the cabin, talking to the woman Honey. He looked over quickly as Striker barked out his name.

"Hog, you still carry them ears, do you?" Striker rasped out a chuckle. "Them you cut off that feller you worked over that time, huh?" Striker opened his mouth wide, his eyebrows raised in question, and his little eyes sparkling with laughter.

"Sold 'em a while back, Gage. Remember? I told you."

The room had quietened at this brief exchange, everyone feeling that there was something more in Striker's question than just idle curiosity.

"Well, maybe you could use another pair?" Striker said, grinning over the words, and with an eye on Honey, who was looking at him with disgust. By God, that filly was a real one, all right. He'd been sharing her with Hog, but by golly, maybe it was time to have it all. At least for the while.

"What you got in mind?" Hog asked, moving over to where Striker was sitting.

"There is a man got a place not so far from here."

"You want his ears, that it?" laughed Hog and swept his eyes around the group as they all took up the laugh.

"Might. Mostly I want some information."

"Shouldn't be too hard to get it," Hog said, with professional ease. "Where's he at?"

"Got a spread down by Shoshone Peak. Not far."

Hog's sweaty face went tight with thought. "You don't mean . . . ?"

"I do!" Striker cut him off fast before he could say Conrad's name, and Hog was brought up short. He reddened a little, but then got back into himself pretty fast. Striker didn't always spell things out, and a man had to be sharp. He felt Honey's eyes on him, but he was able now to handle that, too.

"We'll talk later on it," Striker said. "Meanwhile we'll lay low awhile."

"We gonna hit the railroad, are we?" somebody asked. "You mentioned it back a while."

A grin swept into the bandit leader's face. "We are. We done our practice times. Now we'll go after something big. But it's gonna take some planning."

"Good enough, by God!" somebody said and held up a bottle in toast. "Here's to robbing the goddam railroad deaf, dumb, and blind!"

Striker's grin left his face, but it was still inside him as the men started to file out of the cabin; all except Hog. The girl had moved out to the kitchen.

When the door closed behind the last man, Striker said, "We'll take Conrad up to that cave at the top of the canyon, where the creek narrows. You'll need two more men."

"He's an old bugger; not hard to handle."

"Old? Old, you say?"

"And he's got that game hand."

Striker's grin was not kindly as he looked at Hog Wyatt. "Lemme tell you somethin'. That old man with that game hand is not a man even myself would figure too much to mess with. You know he rode with Whistler. Him and Whistler was a pair, let me tell you. They were like ten! And long as there is breath in that old man, as you call him, he is one you watch yourself with. I taught you, god-damit, Hog. Now you mind me! You take two men, and you mind that man Conrad. If you fuck up, I promise, I personally will take your ears!"

Gage Striker was a man who—as the old saying had it—knew which side his bread was buttered, also who provided the butter and the bread. And so when the rider had arrived from town with the message that his presence was required at a meeting, he didn't hesitate.

"I'll be checking on a few things," he told Hog Wyatt, who was watching him saddle his big steel-dust gelding. "You hold on to what we was talking about till I get back. 'Course, you can be thinking on how you'll be doing it. But stick close here to the cabin, and don't take any shit from Kelly when he gets back from town. He ain't going to be in any special good mood."

"Gotcha." Hog smiled, pleased to be thus deputized as number two, higher than Roan Kelly.

Striker grabbed a handful of mane and his rein

and swung up into the saddle. The steel-dust horse started to throw his head down to buck, but Striker yanked up on his rein, cussing and cutting the animal across the rump and withers with the ends of his lines. After a couple of crow hops the big horse settled down and with Striker standing in the stirrups, they cantered out of the clearing.

They were not a very long way from the town—either Bone City or Riddle Rock being about the same distance from the canyon. But Striker took his time, working a long trail just in case anybody was about who might pick up on his tracks. At one point when he was not far from Shoshone Peak he had an impulse to swing over to Conrad's place, just to bugger that man some; let him know something was coming his way and not knowing when or from where. But he put the impulse aside. His appointment was important, that he knew, and it wouldn't be smart to turn up too late.

He rode through the dying light now as it began leaving the sky to the coming twilight; the late, late afternoon sun squeezing across the land until finally it was over; the day was ended. And it was night, and the cooler air brushed into his eyes, his nose, and he stepped-up the gray horse to a brisker pace.

It was dark when he saw the light in the big house. He came quartering carefully down the long, wide draw that swept right into the edge of the town, coming as he was from the north. Beyond the house he saw the lights of the winking town. And he thought how when he got done with his business he just might slip into town to see a couple of people—maybe some girls. But then caution touched him, plus the memory of Honey Hooligan. Better wait. And what the hell, he had better stuff back at the canyon than anything those moth bags in town had to offer.

He deliberately wiped out thoughts of the girls in town, and also of Honey Hooligan as he neared the first line of fence that ran around the house. He had spotted an outrider when he'd first come in sight of the place, and then another when he was about halfway down the draw. He rode easy, his hand near his gun. The moon was not up and darkness helped, though he wasn't worrying about anybody spotting him. The message had told him his way would be clear. Still it was handy to know that there were two men on duty, on the outside, and likely more inside the house.

He drew rein at the first hitching rail and dismounted, wrapping his lines loosely around the hitch pole; not tying them, just in case a fast departure was necessary.

He didn't walk round to the front of the building, but knocked on the back door, as he had the last time he'd been here. The door opened almost immediately.

"Come in, Striker."

His host closed the door behind him, and then turned up the gas lamp that was in the hall.

"We'll go into my study," Horace Harpe said. "We won't be disturbed. And we can have something to drink and eat while we talk."

"It's what I mean," the boy was saying. "If you'd teach me, then I wouldn't run the risk of getting shot up so easy, like I did with that feller in the saloon."

They were having coffee and pie in the Golden Egg Eatery, following Abel's adventure with Roan Kelly. In the near-paralysis that took over the saloon following the Gunsmith's gun exercise, Clint had hurried the boy outside before anything further could take place. While he had no fear that Kelly would draw on him without thinking twice, he knew the man might well try to get back at Abel.

"I don't want him even to be sure what you look like," he told the boy as they walked quickly down to the Golden Egg. Unfortunately, Abel was taking the opportunity to urge Clint once again to teach him the art of gunfighting.

Clint had expected it. It was always the way whenever someone saw his ability; someone inevitably wanted to learn it. But, as he told Abel now, there was no teaching, that was to say, beyond fundamentals. You either had the reflexes or you didn't.

"My mom used to say something about how if you're the strongest man in the world you don't have to fight anybody. People leave you alone. It's got to be the same if you're the top gunfighter."

Clint was already shaking his head. "That's just where you're wrong, son. I mean, maybe with the strong men it might be like that; but with guns. . . ." He paused, spreading his hands away from the mug of coffee he'd been holding. "The strong man beats somebody up, but the gunman doesn't beat anyone up. He kills. And listen,

Abel—killing is forever.''

"Yeah. I know.''

"Fighting isn't something you might win at if you're hopelessly outclassed. There are almost never any fluke wins. And a fight usually takes time. But with guns, it's once and forever. Think of that. Think it over.''

The boy said nothing to that but stared down at his half-eaten piece of apple pie.

"You don't have any ideas on my dad, I guess,'' he said finally, looking up at Clint, who had been studying him.

"Some thoughts, but nothing that holds firm. I have a strong feeling about the situation, but nothing I'd want to talk over with you or Lorrie at this point. It's too much in the air. What I want is some facts. You see, if he did change his name when he came out here—and a lot of people do, they want to start a new life—it only makes it that much harder. As you know. But think again: Do you really want to find him? Don't you think if he wanted his whereabouts known he would have done something about it?''

"But he might be dead.''

"He might be. But maybe he still wouldn't want his whereabouts known. You see what I'm getting at. What would your dad want?''

"Shit,'' muttered the boy. "I kind of wish I hadn't come out here.''

Clint nodded thoughtfully. "It's a tough one. I know. I feel for both of you.''

"Except, I don't wish I hadn't come,'' Abel said, looking up suddenly, right into Clint Adams' eyes. "I like it here. And . . . in spite of everything—what you say—I want to find out who my father was, if he's still alive. Maybe he's in trouble somewhere, and I could help him. Mister Adams, I really appreciate what you've been doing to help us, but I still. . . ."

Abel stopped talking and looked down at the checkered tablecloth. He was holding his head very low, and Clint wondered if he was fighting tears.

"I'll go on helping you if I can, Abel, and if you'll let me."

The boy was silent, and then Clint knew he was crying. He could tell by the way Abel was gripping his coffee mug, by the tension in his young shoulders, by the way he held his head so that no one would see him.

Clint stopped watching him, even moving in his chair so that Abel would realize he was paying attention to something else. He wanted the boy to have that room for himself. He wanted to get to the bottom of whatever it was going on—Aaron Whistler, Andy Everns, the cache, the recent holdups, the Box Canyon gang; all of it. It was all connected, he knew. And Conrad. And, yes, Horace Harpe.

"The boy was here," Conrad was saying as he stood facing Clint Adams out by the round horse corral. "Told me he was going on up to Killingtown."

"He'd already been there," Clint said.

"That's what I know," Conrad said, and he spat reflectively in the direction of the barn.

"What do you figure he's going up there again for?" Clint asked.

"Dunno. Maybe he thought of something. But hell, there ain't nothin' up there except the weather and some old bodies filled with lead to hold 'em down."

"I am wondering if he maybe did think of something."

But further reflection on the matter was interrupted by Conrad suddenly cocking his head. In the same instant Clint heard the horses.

"Into the timber," snapped Conrad. And they were already running for cover.

They just made it as the first horse and rider came into view.

From their cover in the tall spruce and pine, Clint Adams and Conrad watched the three horsemen ride right up to the ranch house and draw rein.

"You mind that big sonofabitch yonder?" Conrad said, chewing slowly on his plug of tobacco.

"Hog Wyatt. I was at the stage depot when he busted loose with his girl friend."

"Honey Hooligan. Yeah, that is some handful of woman. Too much for that dumb sonofabitch, riding up here all wide like that."

Both watched as one of the men with Hog Wyatt stepped down from his horse and walked up to the cabin and banged on the door. Clint could tell they'd been drinking some—not enough to make them erratic, but sufficient to make them careless.

The two men in the trees waited while no one answered the loud knocking, listened while the three visitors discussed the situation.

"They ain't nobody there," one of the men said.

"You bright sonofabitch," snarled Hog Wyatt.

"You watch yer language there, Hog," the other man snapped back.

"We might as well haul outta here," the third man said.

"We will wait for him," Hog said. "We come to get Conrad, and by God, that is what we are going to do."

"Cover me," Conrad said to Clint, and he stepped out from the line of trees and into full view of the three men. He was holding his Greener .12 gauge, cut down in the barrel for a murderous fire on anyone who invited it.

"There is three of us," Hog Wyatt said, his hand stopping halfway to his holstered side arm. "We could get you sure even with that scatter gun there."

"Mebbe," Conrad said, his lips tight, but himself easy. " 'Ceptin' who'll be the one living to tell Striker about it?"

"Whoever it is will be the one I get," the Gunsmith said, still under cover in the stand of trees.

His voice did the trick. Without further ado, the three men let their hands fall to their sides.

"You get on yer horses," Conrad said. "And you tell Striker next time to send a man for his dirty work. Now get yer asses movin'. I mean right now!"

Clint watched Hog Wyatt's Adam's apple pump a couple of time, while the man's little eyes pin pointed Conrad.

"You can't get away with this shit," Hog said. "We don't take you now, we'll do it later."

Clarence Conrad spat to one side, not taking his

eyes from his three visitors. "Mebbe I cannot get away with it, Wyatt; but this here not only can but is!" And his callused thumb drew back the hammer of the deadly-looking shotgun. All heard the click in the thin mountain air.

"Next time you might not have your friend helpin' you," Hog said as he turned toward his horse and took up the reins.

"There isn't going to be a next time, mister," Conrad said, and his words were as hard as the gun barrel he was pointing. "Fact is, this is next time. Now git!"

Clint waited in the trees until they had ridden back down the trail.

"They'll be back," he said when he came out and watched with Conrad as the three horsemen wound down the side of the mountain toward the river far below.

Conrad nodded. "That is what I know," he said.

"Maybe you better move out for a spell."

"They'll fire my place then."

"They won't right now. Maybe they'll try in a day or two."

Conrad was still watching the riders far below them as they got closer to the river.

"Listen," said Clint. "We have got unfinished business, the both of us."

Conrad sniffed at that, studying it briefly, and then he said, "That is so. And we sure won't get it finished standing about here scratching our asses."

Clint grinned then; he really liked that old man. "Let's go, then."

•　•　•

The early sunlight was washing over the ruined town as the Gunsmith and Clarence Conrad rode in.

"A while since I bin this way," Conrad observed. "Place has sure changed."

"I'll bet." The Gunsmith was walking Duke slowly along what had once been the only street in Killingtown.

"Nobody here," Conrad said.

"But someone has been here," Clint observed, nodding toward some tracks in the ground where it was softer. "Fresh."

Conrad, leaning out of his saddle, nodded. "Day old, I'd allow," he said. "Those three."

"Hog and his buddies."

"And somebody else," Conrad noted.

Clint had already spotted the tracks of the blue roan Abel had been riding.

"Looks like the boy's pony," Conrad said.

The two men walked their horses around the still legible tracks, reading them, trying to piece the story together. And soon it became clear what had happened.

"The kid's gone along with them," the Gunsmith said.

"What do you reckon he come back here for?" Conrad wanted to know. "He was already here, didn't find anything to help him locate his dad, far as I can figure. So what the hell was he doin' here—I mean, again?"

They had both dismounted and were studying the tracks closer; the three Striker men, including Hog Wyatt, and Abel and his blue roan. Evidently, from what both of them could read, Abel had been at the site first, and Hog and his companions had come upon him.

"The boy was here first," Conrad said. "Piecing it from the start, let's say."

Clint nodded. "So why did he come back here? Did he have a reason? He didn't say anything to me along that line, and you say he didn't seem to have anything but curiosity for Killingtown. Nothing clear that would bring him here again. Except maybe just not knowing what else to do."

"And he felt he had to be doing something, is what you're saying," threw in Conrad. "That could be." He nodded in tentative agreement with his own words. "It could be something like that."

The Gunsmith was silent to that. Looking over, Conrad saw him squatting and studying something on the ground. They were at the side of a fallen-down building, on terrain that had formed an alleyway between some scattered lumber and logs and a half-standing building which was even more decomposed.

Suddenly the Gunsmith started to dig into the soft ground with his hands.

"Watcha got?"

The Gunsmith pulled the watch and chain out of the ground by the foundation of one of the buildings.

"Huh." Conrad took it and examined it. "Nothing special. Just a watch," he said. "But that ground there looks like it was just recently covered over. I mean like this here wasn't buried on purpose but just got covered maybe when there was some kind of action going on."

"I am reading that right along with you," Clint

said. "Look! See that outline? Looks like something, maybe someone was lying there." He had been staring hard at the imprint of some kind of weight, and now he raised his head and began following a path where the new grass had been bent and was not yet straightened.

"Something got drug along there," Conrad said.

"Or someone."

"More'n likely I'd say now. It was someone."

They had followed the sign of something being dragged toward a copse of bullberry bushes at the back of the ruined houses.

"Holy shit," muttered Clarence Conrad as they stood looking down at the old man's body. "Looks like he fell over yonder, by the stones there—the foundation—and later was drug here."

"The question is, why?" Clint pushed his hat back on his head as he stood looking down at the body.

It was an older man they were looking at. And it didn't appear he had died from any sort of violence.

"Looks like a old prospector, somebody like that," Conrad observed. "Died natural. Least, that's what it looks like now."

"But somebody found him. Maybe later? And dragged him into the bushes." Clint shook his head, wondering. "Why?" And then something caught his eye, and he kneeled down.

"Is there a mine near here?" he asked without looking up.

"Used to be the Red Dog. But it was a fluke. It ran out almost before it got started."

"Gold." And Clint looked up at the other man. "See this?" He pointed to the old man's clothing, brushing his fingers along his shirt.

In the strong morning sunlight the glint of gold dust was unmistakable.

A long, low whistle came out of Clarence Conrad's pursed lips as he knelt down beside the body of the old man and followed Clint Adams' pointing finger.

"The Red Dog hasn't been operating in one helluva good while," Conrad said. "And this feller is not easy to recognize since he has been dead some while, but I do believe I seen him. Used to come into town now and again, from his prospecting the hills hereabouts. Had a mule named Gabriel. By God, looks like he struck it somewheres."

"Where would you think likely?" Clint asked.

Conrad's forehead wrinkled. "Could be any place, maybe even near the Red Dog."

"Would you say no if I suggested it might actually be the Red Dog?"

"No, but how do you figure that?"

"I'm guessing. But I've an idea that somebody knows where there's a good vein, maybe even bonanza, and maybe even in the Red Dog. Actually, it doesn't matter too much. The point is, this man knew where the gold is. Let's say he died of natural cause. Hog and his men found him."

"And pulled him over here to keep him out of sight."

"Maybe even Abel Everns found him first. Look at those prints back there."

Clint stood up and looked down at the old prospector. "You want to know what I'm thinking?"

"I believe I know. And if it's the same as me, everybody's been off on a wild goose chase."

"I'll tell you something else I think," Clint said.

"I am sure listening."

"Somebody—I won't say the name yet—but somebody arranged for Striker to break out of Laramie. Somebody had the old gang waiting for him when he got here. Somebody has known all along that there isn't any Aaron Whistler cache, but there is a gold mine."

"You're saying the whole deal has been a fake."

"A fake, a feint in one direction while the real move has been toward something else. Toward some real money."

There was almost a grin on Clarence Conrad's face as he looked squarely at his companion now. "I am reading it right along with you, my friend. Hell, I feel twenty years younger. Let's cut leather!"

TEN

"Well, well . . . !" Striker regarded Abel Everns with amusement on his wet face. "Interestin' to have you drop in on us, young feller." He kept his eyes moving up and down Abel, who was standing in front of him with a puzzled look on his face. Hog Wyatt, minus his recent pair of companions, stood to one side, not only pleased with himself for bringing in evidence of his zeal, but relieved for having something to offer in place of his failure with Conrad.

"What's yer name, boy?"

"Abel Everns. What's your name?"

"You can call me Striker. Now listen . . ." They were in the cabin, and Striker, seated as usual on his empty nail keg, leaned forward. "You tell me what you were doing back there where Hog here says you was, and why."

"I don't know that that's any of your business, mister," Abel said.

Before he had reached the end of what he was saying, Striker was in movement. The next thing Abel knew he was on the floor with the side of his head feeling as though he'd been hit with a rock.

The big man was standing over him, his legs, like pillars spread apart, ready for action with fist or gun. "Get up, and start over. I don't expect no

159

sass from you, sonny. I ask you a question, I want
a answer!''

With his head ringing, and pretty much fright-
ened, Abel pulled himself to his feet. He was diz-
zy, but anger took over and steadied him as he saw
the big grin on Hog Wyatt's face.

"I've been looking for someone, a relative of
mine, from back in Indiana," he said after a moment of regaining his breath.

"Up here? At Killingtown? For Chrissake,
there ain't nobody here but snakes and coyotes.
What were you doing with that old man?''

"I told him"—he nodded in the direction of
Hog Wyatt—"I told him what I was doing. That
old man was dead when I found him. I never saw
him before in my life."

Striker had reseated himself on the keg. "Boy,
if you be lying to me I will kill you—but slow."

"I'm telling you what happened!"

"Sassy, ain't he," observed Hog. "He was like
that all the way here."

"Shut up!" snapped Striker. "I got questions
for you, too, on why you didn't bring the one here
I sent you for. You stupid sonofabitch!"

It was at this point that Abel noticed the girl
standing in the doorway to the other room.

"Why don't you slow down and give the kid
something to eat?" Honey said. "Can't you see he
looks hungry?" She glared insolently at Striker,
who was scratching his crotch.

"Boy, who was this person you bin looking for?
He got a name?"

"Andy Everns."

"He somebody to you? A relative?"

"My father."

"Well, I never heard of him. You ever hear of such a name, Hog?"

"No."

Striker nodded toward Honey without looking at her. "All right then, get him something. And you, Hog. You don't let him out of your sight. I don't want anybody around who knows how to get into this place or even knows we are here."

"I blindfolded him," Hog said, looking smug.

"I don't give a shit what you did. You do what I tell you!"

"You keeping me prisoner here?" Abel asked.

"Boy, you are a smart one," Striker said.

And then Abel said the wrong thing. "You'd better let me go. My friends will come for me if I ain't back."

"Who? What friends? You don't look to me like you're from this here country."

Abel stood in his silence, saying nothing, realizing too late his mistake.

But this time Striker's voice was not hard, not threatening. He said, "Who was that old man Hog found you with? You sure he wasn't your Paw?"

"I am sure."

"Who was your Paw? You ain't from around here. What was your Paw, this Andy feller, doing out here?"

"I dunno."

"But you say he was here—around Bone City and Riddle Rock."

"That's right."

"You come out here all by yourself, did you—I

mean from back East, like Hog said."

There was the barest hesitation before Abel said, "Yes." But it was enough to tell Striker.

"Boy, you are lying to me. You are lying to Striker. I warned you about that."

At that moment Honey Hooligan came back into the room. "I've got something for him in the kitchen."

Striker seemed to think on it for a moment, and then he said, "Good enough. Get him set, and then come back here. I got something I want to say to you."

When she had left, he turned to Hog. "You and me, Hog, will see why the hell you didn't bring Conrad in."

"He had that sonofabitch with him, the one they call the Gunsmith. The one that was at the stage depot when Honey got me loose from them two deputies."

Honey had returned to the room now. "You'll tell me all about it when I'm through with her," Striker said. "Now git."

He turned to the girl. "You find out what he was doing up here. I don't believe him. He's holding something back. Like when I asked him was he alone. You get something from him I might show some favor to you."

Honey simply regarded him with the loathing she could not conceal, and indeed made no attempt to, as she turned and went back into the kitchen where Abel was seated at the table, looking at the plate of food before him.

In the other room Striker was staring into space with a puzzled look on his face.

• • •

Clint and Conrad had ridden their horses hard and had reached the opening of the box canyon by late afternoon.

"Chances are they'll have outriders watching the way in and the way out," Conrad said.

"You remember the setup well, do you?" Clint asked. "I figured it had been a while since you were around this part of the country."

"It is a long time," Conrad said. "But I am getting the feel of it."

Clint dropped his eyes to his companion's waist. Conrad was packing the holstered six-gun he had seen hanging on the mantle over the fireplace in his cabin.

"Figured I could use all the armaments I had," Conrad said, noticing Clint's look. "This here was Aaron's gun. He give it to me when he was . . . going. Told him I already had a gun and didn't need it. He said 'You never know. There might come a time you'll wish you had it.' Maybe this is such a time."

"Might make dry camp yonder," Clint said. "And go in the canyon after dark a bit, or early morning."

"That'd be a good time—the morning. But mind you, Striker will have this place closely guarded. We always did in the old days."

They had dismounted now at the place designated by Clint and had spread out their ground covers and bedrolls.

"Do you think Striker will hurt the boy?" Clint asked.

"Depends. The bad thing will be if he finds out who he is."

"I've been figuring the same thing. So I'm going in to have a look-see when it's dark."

"You know, I was figuring the same thing," Conrad said.

"How far inside the canyon will the cabin be?" Clint asked.

"I'd judge a half mile. It's well inside. But we got to remember it's been a lot of years since I was here. The growth will be different, and there could be other changes, too."

Both of them had squatted to open their bedding and remove extra ammo and food. Clint opened a can of peaches and brought out some beef jerky. He offered what he had to Conrad.

"Can you draw and shoot with your left hand now?" Clint asked.

"Some. It ain't like my right used to be. But it is better than nothing. Least the shooting is. The draw is something else. Never was much good with my left, and I ain't any great shakes right now. But. . ." He let it hang, shrugging, sniffing as he took the beef jerky and started to chew on it.

When they were finished their meal they had a smoke, each easing back into himself to reflect on the situation.

"Where is the Red Dog located exactly?" Clint asked after a long moment of studying the aspects of their problem.

"Up by Sawyer Creek, past Harpe's place on the North Fork road."

"Handy," Clint said.

"Handy for Harpe, you're saying?"

"Handy for Harpe. It may sound crazy to you, Conrad, but I am having thoughts about our friend Mr. Harpe. And one of those thoughts is how come Gage Striker was able to get out of Laramie; and I understand that at the time of his escape he was supposed to be in solitary confinement—making it all that much harder to escape."

"You got a point there, I think," Conrad said, nodding his gray head sagely.

"I have got another point," Clint said. "And it is this. How come there hasn't been any lawman around checking on whether or not Striker headed back to this country after he busted out? Wouldn't you think there'd be a marshal or two looking for such a man around his old haunts, his old stomping grounds? But there has been nobody, as far as I've been able to discover."

"You telling me that you figger there's a connection between Striker and Horace Harpe? That is sure crazy as hell, Adams." Conrad spat quickly at a clump of sage brush. "Though, on th'other hand, maybe it ain't." And he pursed his long lips, nodding his head thoughtfully a few times, his eyes moving all over Clint Adams' face. "Maybe it ain't," he added.

Clint stood up. "Should be dark enough now."

"Let's go, then," Conrad said. And he touched the six-gun at his side as he walked toward his groundhitched saddle pony.

It took Abel a long time to get the window open, using the jackknife Honey Hooligan had slipped him while he was eating the meal she had prepared for him in the kitchen. After which

Striker had come in and told her where to take the
boy, to a shack which was more lean-to than
building, since it joined onto the rear of the log
cabin and was mostly hidden in brush. It had the
small window, which gave into the thick stand of
trees, and the door, which was firmly locked from
the outside. But she had slipped him the knife,
then leaned forward to whisper that Striker was
about to go somewhere, and that she would keep
Hog occupied, and if necessary, any others who
might be set up as guards.

Abel had tasted his fear sweeping all through
him, but he held himself still. He was afraid, but
he wasn't lost in his fear. And so when Hog Wyatt
locked him into the shack, he immediately examined his quarters. The woman had also given
him some matches so he was able to take a quick
look at his surroundings. Then he went to work on
the window. It was small, but he figured he could
squeeze through it if he could manage to get it
open.

Meanwhile, inside the cabin, Striker had taken
his leave, and Hog and Honey were alone. There
were sentries outside, of course, and there were
outriders beyond the cabin, even outside the box
canyon. Striker was taking no chances, especially
now, especially since the boy.

It took Abel a couple of hours to get the window frame loose. He had to work slowly and
quietly, for it was tiring work as well as noisy if he
wasn't careful. But finally after what seemed to
him an endless time, the window was loose in its
frame. The question now was whether he could
squeeze through.

He had just started to take the frame out when he heard someone at the door. He swiftly pushed it back in and just made it back to the horse blanket, which was his bed, on the dirt floor of the shack.

The lantern preceded his visitor, throwing its light all over the walls and the old sacking that was piled in a corner. The boy lay with his eyes slightly open so that he could see but still appear to be sleeping.

To his relief, it was the girl Honey who entered. At first she was alone, but then the man Hog came in, and Abel's hopes sank.

"You hungry, boy? You want something to eat?" Honey asked, standing over him as she held the coal oil lamp high.

He stirred, pretending to come out of sleep. He wasn't hungry but he said, "Yes. I am hungry."

"Bring you something, then," she muttered, and without anything further, the two of them left, locking the door behind them.

Abel continued to lie there on his blanket, visualizing his escape, wondering what he could possibly use as a weapon. There was nothing in the shack, so it would have to be whatever he could pick up outside in the way of a club.

When he heard someone at the door he opened his eyes, and turning on his side, drew his legs up so that he would be in a position to rise quickly if necessary. It was Honey carrying a tray, followed again by Hog. She set the tray on the ground near Abel, there being no furniture at all in the shack. Hog followed her all the way inside the shack, carrying the lantern.

Squatting with the tray, Honey set it down beside the boy. Now, with her eyes on his face she said, "Hog, I forgot that can of peaches. Get it, will you, it's on the table in the kitchen. Leave the lamp while you go."

With a coarse mumble of irritation, the man set the lamp on the ground and left.

"Your horse is just below the cabin hitched to the corral. Can you ride bareback? You won't have time to saddle him."

"I'll do it," Abel said, sitting up.

"He's only got a hackamore on him. Don't waste any time. I hope you used the knife."

"The window's free. I'll make it out."

"Give me about fifteen, twenty minutes with him," she said. "Make it fifteen."

She stood up just as Hog came in with the can of peaches.

Abel waited a few moments after they had left; silent, listening, and then he tried the window. It was loose enough to come out easily. But he waited, remembering how she'd wanted fifteen minutes. She had said nothing about any guards about the place, and he assumed that she hadn't spoken of that from not knowing the layout any better than he did. So he would have to be doubly careful.

Clint and Conrad had seen the horseman riding out of the canyon.

"That is damn close," Conrad said softly as they watched the figure cantering past them. They had just made it into the trees.

"He's in a hurry, that's why we heard him,"

Clint said. "You know him."

"Couldn't see much even with the moon," Conrad said. "But I'll give odds it was Striker. And that's a rum one."

"How so?"

"He's the kind who always has men with him."

"Then he's likely on something special," Clint said. "Like a visit maybe, huh?"

"I am thinking the same thing. Maybe one of us ought to follow."

"It's got to be something important if he's heading into town by himself, meaning he's doing it secretly," Clint said.

"Do you figger he's figured out about the boy?"

"If he has, that means the girl is also in trouble." He reached down and touched the butt of his six-gun, and looked at Conrad, whose outline he could just see in the dim light.

"We'll be split," Conrad said, thinking right along with the Gunsmith.

"Exactly. We'll go for the kid first, then."

They rode through the trees, Conrad leading the way, though not too sure, since it had been some years since his last journey to the canyon. At one point he drew rein, and when Clint came up beside him he said he thought there should be outriders ahead.

"We're coming in on the cabin now. Aaron used to keep men up there and over yonder." He pointed.

"You figure Striker would follow the same."

"Ten will get you twenty on that."

It was just then that Clint held up his hand. The

moon had risen, but for some moments had been behind a cloud, and now it was suddenly out, lighting the whole landscape. Both men heard the rock tumbling, a rock very likely kicked by a horse's hoof. And then they saw him.

"It's the kid," Conrad whispered.

"We'd better make sure he isn't followed."

They sat their horses, each of them reaching forward to cover their animal's muzzle with a hand to prevent any nickering recognition as the rider approached. They could see Abel quite clearly now.

"Hear anything?" Conrad asked after a moment as Abel passed across their view of the trail.

"No, but let's wait."

Suddenly, just as Abel was out of view, Hog Wyatt's voice cut through the night air. "I've got you covered with a scatter gun, kid. Don't try to get away."

Clint kicked Duke closer to Conrad. "We'll get on up to the cabin. He won't hurt the kid, or he would have shot first and spoken afterwards."

Conrad nodded and together they moved their horses swiftly along the trail to the cabin.

"We'll come in from the back," Conrad said after a moment or so. "He's probably got his men all around, though 'course some could be in town drinking."

"I want to make it into the cabin," Clint said. And as they came in sight of the log house he said, "I'm going right in. You stay by that shack there and cover me with the scatter gun."

And without further words he kicked Duke into a fast walk, and as luck would have it, a cloud blocked the light of the moon at just that moment. The Gunsmith felt like muttering a prayer at that, knowing as he did that the odds were stacked all the way against them pulling off what he had in mind.

Well, almost all the way, he told himself as he guided Duke into the trees behind the cabin, dismounted, and groundhitched him and then started toward the back door.

The moon was still hidden, so he still had the cover of darkness to help him. He took only enough time at the back door to ensure the quiet that he needed. It was a long and painful moment for he expected Hog Wyatt to come pounding in with Abel at any minute.

He heard the horses just as he managed to get the back door open without making any noise. In an instant he was inside the kitchen. There was no sound coming from the front room, but he knew somebody, maybe more than one person, was there. He waited, listening for the slightest sound or movement. At the same time, the fear that had been in him from the moment he had seen Striker riding out, added to by the capture of Abel by Hog Wyatt, was almost overwhelming him. It was not so much a fear, really, as it was a very deep concern, yet close to becoming a strong fear if he allowed it to. It was simply that he knew Lorrie was in danger. He knew it. Yet he had made the choice, for he felt the boy was in worse danger. So he had gambled.

None of this was at the front of his mind as he waited in the kitchen of the log cabin, yet it was there nonetheless. Like a presence. Still, he knew he must not allow it to get any stronger or it would affect his action. And now, at this very moment, he needed to be as free as he'd ever been in his life. And so, too, did the old man waiting outside by the shack with his cut down shotgun, his game hand, and his sixty years.

The Gunsmith was no stranger to this moment. In a way he knew it was where he really lived; and he knew, too, that it could be where he died. That special moment when a man's life and his death were in the same place.

ELEVEN

This time he wasn't expected, and it was not Harpe who opened the door for him when he knocked. It was the woman. Striker had seen her once before, and he had been smitten.

"I will tell Mr. Harpe you are here," Andrea said, pointing to a chair in a short hallway.

It was a while before she came back, and Striker was beginning to fidget. He was not a man who favored being kept waiting, not even by people of Horace Harpe's rank. But his surliness fled the moment he saw the woman again. Each time he saw her she looked better. Well, if only he had the time, he was thinking as his eyes followed her quivering buttocks down the hall to the door with the large brass knob. She gave a single knock and then opened the door, walking in ahead of Striker, then standing aside to let him pass. He felt his head swim as he inhaled her perfume. But in the next instant he was brought back to reality by the hard, cold voice of Harpe.

"I didn't know we had a meeting set up, Striker. What is it you want?"

Striker had not been prepared for this sort of reception, but he was not a successful outlaw for nothing. His scowling eyebrows, his jutting jaw, his iron backbone swept such discourtesy aside as he said, "That kid, the one lookin' for his old man, he's Whistler's kid. I'll bet my wad on it."

"I am ahead of you on that, Striker," Harpe said easily, and with less rough words. "I have already figured that out. Why? I take it you've met up with him."

"The boys caught him snoopin' around Killingtown and brought him in."

Harpe seemed to unbend a little now as he reached for glasses and a bottle inside his desk. Placing a glass in front of his visitor, he uncorked and poured.

"What was he snooping around for?"

"Told me he was looking for his Paw."

"I know that—I am aware of all that. What was he really doing?"

"I dunno. But here's what the boys found." Striker, angry again at the way Harpe was treating him, allowed an appreciable pause to come between them. But he swiftly realized that Harpe was up to his game. Horace Harpe was completely at ease as he waited for Striker to continue.

"Hog and the boys found that old prospector Willie, the one used to work way back at that strike—the Red Dog. Before your time that was. But it was a number-one strike, going to make everybody a million, but then it ran out all sudden-like."

"I have heard of the Red Dog," Harpe said. "So what was this old man doing?"

"He was dead."

"Dead!"

"Dead, but not from bullets. Old age, something like that. He died natural, Hog said. No marks. He wasn't beat up or anything."

"So what does all this mean? Is this any reason for you to take the great risk of riding in here to see me on the spur of the moment without any notice!''

"Listen, there was gold dust on him. He might of died natural-like, but he died rich."

"I see." Harpe sat back in his chair, lifting his glass as he took it all in. Willie dead, an accident apparently, that is to say, as far as his plans were concerned. And so, inconvenient as hell. Willie had been watching the mine, along with the other oldster, Finlayson. He wondered where Finlayson was. The question was, did Striker suspect anything. It didn't look like it.

"You figger that vein might not of run out?" Striker was asking.

"There's no way of my knowing anything about it," Harpe said. "But I might look into it."

Striker shifted in his chair and took a generous pull at his drink. "That kid, you know he might know something about where his old man hid his cache."

"I am thinking the very same thing, Striker. And I was, in fact, about to say so."

"I can whip it out of him easy enough."

"Do you really believe he might know something? He must have been awfully young, if we're thinking of the same boy, when his father and he were together."

"He might of heard something, seen something. A map," said Striker. "One way to find out anyways." He stood up.

"Sit down, Striker. We are not finished."

The words came across the desk like ice.

Striker was afraid of no man, and he was not afraid of Horace Harpe, but those cold, hard words put him back down in his seat.

"There is no point in being hasty, Striker. And please do not forget that you are—uh—here, as it were, under my protection."

He had forgotten that, and in the face of it he now remained silent.

"Ride on back to the canyon," Harpe said. "Keep the boy there. Do not harm him in any way. I've an idea I shall try out."

"Hog said he had a sister also come out here," Striker said.

Horace Harpe held up the palm of his hand. "Enough. Enough." And he stood up and escorted Striker to the door. With his hand on the knob, he paused. "Oh, and Striker. Next time, do not forget our—uh—agreement, or your instructions, if that might be a better wording—that you only come to see me in the event of an emergency. This was certainly no emergency."

Striker said nothing. But he was not happy. He was muttering to himself as he left the house.

Horace Harpe knew it. He had sized his associate's temper well. Yes, it might be the moment for a change. Certainly with the mine coming into the picture. He had been lucky in keeping that silent, or rather, not so lucky as clever. But he knew it couldn't remain a secret any longer. It was time for him to act. The papers were in order. Fortunately Willie and Finlayson had each signed their shares over to him just within the past week. It was unfortunate old Willie had died so publicly, but what could you do. He—as soon as the papers were cleared by the law—would be in the clear. He was in the clear now, with full title to the Red Dog. It had been close, but by using his head, he had managed to keep the news of the new vein secret. And moreover, he had a strong healthy team of gunmen at his private disposal. And of course, the question of the other, third partner, need never come up. Willie and Finlayson were the survivors, their partner was long dead, and nobody had to be any the wiser.

Horace Harpe was smiling as he started out of his study. Things were working out well. And moreover, he could, as it were, combine business with pleasure. Surely it was time to deal with Lorrie Everns. It was the propitious moment, in a word. And what was more, the girl was attractive. Not in the same way as his present paramour, but he was sure Lorrie Everns could be refreshing. And it was certainly the moment to conclude this stage of his business enterprise. It was, in short, the moment to strike, to make his final move to take over.

The Gunsmith had expected the men to be more cautious, but perhaps it was that without the presence of Striker they inevitably let down. In any event, they neglected to come in the back door as well as the front, always a sensible maneuver when trouble was in the air.

This proved a bonus for the Gunsmith, who simply waited until they were all in the front room of the cabin and then stepped in.

In one glance he took in Abel, Hog, Roan Kelly, and Honey Hooligan. Undoubtedly there were other men about, but it would be up to Conrad to handle them with his Greener .12 gauge.

Both Roan and Hog went for their guns, but this time Clint didn't shoot the gun out of Roan Kelly's hand, but waiting until the man had

cleared leather, he drew and fired one shot right
through Roan Kelly's neck. The man was dead as
he tumbled to the floor. In that split instant, Hog
Wyatt dropped his gun to the ground and threw
up his hands.

"I'm unarmed!" The words came out of his
strangling throat as he stared in fascination and
horror at the Gunsmith's shooting.

The Gunsmith withheld his fire, but he had
taken his attention off Honey Hooligan, who now
entered the room, swept the gun into her hand,
and shot Hog Wyatt in the head, killing him instantly. Then she threw the gun at the Gunsmith's
feet.

"The sonofabitch had it coming to him," she
said. "If I'd had any sense at all I would have
stayed with Horace. Cold fish that he was!"

But Clint Adams didn't waste any time in dis-
cussing the merits or demerits of the killing of Hog
Wyatt by his now ex-lover. The shots had been
heard outside for he heard somebody shouting out
in the yard.

Quickly shooting out the light, he dove for the
back door, yelling at Abel to follow him.

In the next instant they felt the night air on their
faces as, followed by Honey Hooligan, they
charged out of the cabin.

"Over here," called out Conrad who was standing with Duke and his own buckskin pony.

Meanwhile, Honey had called to Abel to follow
her to the corral where the blue roan was hitched,
still saddled and bridled. The four of them
pounded down the trail leading away from the
cabin, with Conrad ahead, guiding them. Shouts,

bullets, and curses came singing after them, but no one was hit.

But the gang was mounting up, yet without a leader they were falling swiftly into disarray. It became almost immediately evident that they were mounting the pursuit simply out of habit and reaction. And so the four soon outdistanced them, as Conrad led them on a long, circuitous, and almost forgotten trail which the bandits apparently didn't know or anyway didn't care too much about.

At last they were out of the canyon and in the clear. But Clint Adams didn't allow them to slacken their pace. He was thinking of Lorrie, a sitting target for Horace Harpe or Striker, or both.

They had ridden hard, and well into the deep night before Clint ordered a halt.

"We've lost 'em," Conrad said. "Though it don't mean they'll give up, even without Hog or Roan Kelly."

They had stopped by a small creek, well beyond the box canyon, and fairly close to Bone City. The horses were blowing, and Clint ordered a dry camp where they could rest themselves and their mounts before riding into town. Hardly a word had been spoken during the race away from the log cabin in the canyon, and now for several moments the silence continued as each one settled down in a small area that was protected by trees.

"We'll take a couple of hours," Clint said. "I'll be watch."

"And myself," added Conrad. "We'll split it, young feller."

Clint nodded at that. "But you two sleep." He was studying Abel and Honey to see what effect the evening's violence had had on them. But both of them seemed to be bearing up well. He had noticed as they rode how the woman had taken a slightly protective air toward the boy, and he realized that it was she who had helped him escape.

"Will Lorrie be all right?" It was the first Abel had spoken since their escape from the cabin.

"I'm sure she'll be all right," Clint said.

"But where are we heading for now?" the boy asked.

"Bone City."

"But what then?" asked Honey, speaking also for the first time since the canyon.

"Striker will follow. For all we know, he might even be there ahead of us. We'll have to handle that as we get to it," Clint said.

"And Harpe," the girl added. "There is Horace to deal with. You know he's into something big. I don't know the details, but it's something to do with an old gold mine."

"Tell me something," Clint said suddenly, looking right at the girl in the moonlight. "Are you still connected to Harpe?"

She shook her head. "That's a funny thing to say. I took up with Hog, as everybody knows. Except he turned out to be a crazy beast. You want to see something?" And before he could answer, she had pulled open her shirt to reveal her breasts. "I don't know if you can see the burns from his cigar in this light."

Clint watched the shining tears of outrage that stood in her eyes. "I'm not sorry I killed him. I'd do it again! I—I just don't have such good luck with men, it appears.'' And she dropped her head, buttoning her shirt. ''No, I'm not with Horace.''

''Hog needed killing long back,'' Conrad said. ''Besides, you helped all of us get out of there.''

She stood there in front of the three of them, crying silently, but with her head unbowed.

Abel turned to the Gunsmith then. ''She helped me get out of there,'' he said.

''I know. I know her,'' Clint said.

And for the rest of the moment there was silence among them. Nothing else needed to be said.

Finally Clint said, ''Better turn in for a spell. We'll need what rest we can get.''

''I wish I had a gun,'' Abel said softly as the moon came again from behind a thin cloud and the night was brighter. ''I bet we're going to have a fight.''

Nobody said anything to that, and he stood alone in the silence that followed his simple words. Conrad and Clint were looking at each other, and while neither said anything to the other, something passed.

Then Conrad spoke. ''Here, boy.'' And he unbuckled the big blue Navy Colt that he'd had around his waist and that had been hanging from the peg on his fireplace back at his ranch. ''I reckon this belongs to yourself now.''

Clint stood picket for the first hour or so, and when he moved over to where Conrad was lying on his blanket, he found the old man already awake. They moved silently out to where they had tied the horses.

''I'll be riding in,'' Clint said.

"Why'n't you wait and we'll go with you?"

"It's easier one man alone. You come on in with those two and then look for me. I could be at Harpe's house, or who knows where."

"I'll find you."

"But get Abel and the woman over to Lorrie at Mrs. Roman's."

Conrad nodded.

Now, riding toward the town, Clint began to piece the picture together from the various bits he'd been holding: Striker's easy escape with no follow-up from the law, the Whistler cache, Horace Harpe's hiring him as a "private policeman," the old prospector out at Killingtown. And, as he had suspected for some while, everything was connected in some way with Harpe. And it was toward Harpe's house that he now rode.

Dawn was just touching the sky along the eastern mountains as he came to the top of the long draw that led down to the big house of Horace Harpe.

He knew that it was inevitable that he would be seen. The careful location of the house prevented any approach that wasn't visible. And so he simply rode down, quartering his horse down the long draw, with his right hand close to his holstered six-gun, and not too far from his belly gun beneath his shirt at his waist.

He spotted the two outriders immediately, but they kept their distance. At the same time he was pretty sure someone in the house would have also seen him. He didn't think anyone would yet know about the action out at the box canyon. But it would be about pretty soon; of that he was certain. He had decided to play it straight. He was still Harpe's "policeman" after all, and he was riding in with his report.

He rode right up to the front of the house and dismounted, wrapping his reins lightly around the hitch rail, and then walking up to the door.

It opened almost immediately to his knock, and Andrea stood before him in a rust-colored silk blouse and tight-fitting riding breeches.

Her eyes were serious as she looked at him. Clint felt she was trying to give him a message, but she said nothing aloud at any rate, as she led him down the hall to Harpe's study and knocked on the door.

He didn't hear anyone answer the knock, but Andrea opened the door and stood aside for him to enter.

Horace Harpe was sitting behind his desk, while to the Gunsmith's left rear he felt, then saw, the burly figure of Striker standing by a window.

"Good morning, Adams," Harpe said, in a voice tinged with light irony. "Rather early for a call, but welcome. Have a seat."

"I'll stand," Clint said. "Just dropped in to bring you up on the latest action."

"Good. But do sit down."

In almost the same instant Clint heard the horses. They were coming in fast.

"It's some of the boys," Striker said from the window. "And they got Conrad with them and the kid and the woman."

"Woman?" Harpe cocked an eye.

"Honey Hooligan."

"What about Hog Wyatt and Kelly?" Harpe asked.

"They're dead," the Gunsmith said. "It's part

of what I came to tell you, Harpe." And to his surprise he saw some of the color leave Harpe's face.

But before Harpe could speak, there was a knock at the door.

"Striker!" Harpe's voice broke hard into the room.

But the Gunsmith lapped him. "Hold it!"

Striker was already stroking his gun from its smooth holster, as the Gunsmith drew and shot him right between the eyes.

He had Horace Harpe fully covered as the door burst open and the three box canyon men entered with Conrad and Abel Everns.

"Drop your guns," snapped Conrad, instantly sizing the situation. "He'll kill Harpe. You can take a look at Striker."

The three were not foolhardy, and with their leader gone, they knew time had gone with him.

"I have the girl, Adams," Harpe said, his face almost chalk white now.

"Get her," Clint said, with a pang of doom in his heart. He could tell Harpe was going all the way.

"We can make a deal, Adams. I'll give you a good share of the mine."

"Whistler's share?"

"I don't. . . ."

"Cut it out. I know he was in it with the two prospectors. It had to be that with the nonsense about a hidden cache so obvious."

"You sayin' there is no cache?" Conrad showed his surprise by moving his mouth and jaw around vigorously, as though chewing at something.

"That's right. Even Striker didn't know, did he, Harpe?"

"Nobody knew. How did you guess? How did you find out, God damn you!"

"Striker went along with his escape thinking he was going to find Whistler's loot and also get even with Conrad. But you had bigger game."

"Dammit! I asked you how you found out!"

"Why, how did I find out, you're asking?" Clint Adams was the picture of innocence as he looked at the angry Horace Harpe. "That was easy."

"What the hell do you mean!" Harpe was furious, almost getting up from his chair but managing to restrain himself by gripping the edge of his desk. "God damn you, Adams! How did you find out? I demand that you tell me!"

"It was very easy," Clint said, speaking with maddening calm. "You told me. Everything you've said and done told me."

Harpe's face was a picture of total incredulity. For an instant Clint thought he looked mad, insane. He started to stand up but sank back into his chair.

At last he managed to speak. "I—I've got the girl, Adams. You will do what I say."

Clint turned to the three men who had brought Abel and Conrad into the room. "Where's the girl? Where's Honey?"

"She's with the other woman outside," one of them said. "She ain't gonna cause trouble."

"You go get her, and you get Miss Everns, too."

"Who?"

"Right now!"

He looked at Harpe, who was sunk in his chair, his face drained of color.

"All right, Adams," he managed to say, the words coming on his breath.

There was a silence in the room for several moments as someone went for the two women. When they heard them out in the corridor, through the open door, Harpe started to speak.

"I think a drink is in order, Adams." And without further ado he reached to his desk for the bottle and glasses. "I believe we're all in need of something."

Clint Adams had been looking at Striker, lying facedown on the floor. Then he turned to Abel. "That's the man who killed your father. He shot him in the back."

The boy looked at him, saying nothing.

"I'll tell you all about it later, or maybe Conrad will."

"What happened to your gun, boy?" Conrad said. "That one I give you back at the creek."

"He took it," Abel said, nodding toward one of the box canyon gunmen.

When Clint looked at the man, he unbuckled Aaron Whistler's big Navy Colt from his waist and tossed it to the boy.

Abel held the holstered gun and cartridge belt in his hands for a moment and then strapped it around his waist.

Meanwhile, Clint had not taken his eyes off Harpe, who was pouring whiskey into three glasses, for himself, Clint, and Conrad.

"That is your dad's gun, Abel," Conrad said.

Abel looked at him, puzzled, letting it come in slowly. He reached to his side and felt the gun and slowly drew it. It was a big gun, heavy, powerful. He hefted it in his hand.

"Can I keep it?" he said.

"I already give it to you," Conrad said.

At that moment the box canyon man who had gone for the two women brought them into the room, and Horace Harpe picked up the whiskey bottle and reached down to return it to his bottom desk drawer.

The Gunsmith had been covertly watching him all along, not showing his awareness of the other, but nonetheless following Harpe's every move. And when Horace Harpe came up with the big .45 in his hand, Clint Adams was quicker and had already drawn his own firearm.

The crash of his Colt double-action blended perfectly with the explosion of Aaron Whistler's big Navy Colt, which Abel fired at his side, while Harpe's bullet didn't even leave its gun.

"Jesus!" said Clarence Conrad. "You both shot him!" And he was staring hard at Abel Everns, who was still holding his father's gun.

After a moment the boy said, "He wasn't the man who killed my father, was he."

"No, son, he wasn't," Conrad said. "But you shot the man who helped him get away with it. And, by God, for my money that's real close."

As luck would have it, Mrs. Roman was visiting elsewhere in town when Clint stopped by. At the same time, Abel was up at Conrad's ranch enjoying his time with the man who had known his father.

"What will you do now?" he asked Lorrie as she brought him a cup of tea in the parlor.

"I guess go back home. But I don't know about Abel. He's a man now. I suspect he'll stay out here, probably with Mr. Conrad."

"When will you be going?" Clint asked, and at the sight of her hesitation, his passion grew swiftly.

"I don't feel in any particular hurry," she said with a small smile. "What about yourself? Isn't it time for you to be getting along?"

"Getting along?"

"I don't see you as settling down. I don't know that you're that type. But, of course, that's not my business."

"What is your business?" he asked. "What would you like to do?"

She seemed to hesitate and sat there in her chair looking at him. Presently she said, "I'd like to show you." And she stood up.

His erection was at its limit as he followed her upstairs.

They didn't speak as she locked her bedroom door. Nor did either of them say anything as he began slowly to undress her.

But he felt the tears on her face as he entered her. "Are you all right?" he asked.

"I've never been happier in my life," she said as he pushed deeper inside her and their bodies began to move together in unison.

"Neither have I," Clint said.

And what he said was true, for when it was like this, when it was this sweet, it was like the very first time, the very best, and the only time. That of course didn't stop either of them from repeating the wonderful moment throughout the night— again and again.